For more than forty years,
Yearling has been the leading name
in classic and award-winning literature
for young readers.

Yearling books feature children's
favorite authors and characters,
providing dynamic stories of adventure,
humor, history, mystery, and fantasy.

Trust Yearling paperbacks to entertain,
inspire, and promote the love of reading
in all children.

Mudville

Kurtis Scaletta

A Yearling Book

Copyright © 2009 by Kurtis Scaletta

Visit us on the Web! www.randomhouse.com/kids

Educators and librarians, for a variety of teaching tools, visit us at www.randomhouse.com/teachers

The Library of Congress has cataloged the hardcover edition of this work as follows:
Scaletta, Kurtis.
Mudville / Kurtis Scaletta.
p. cm.
Summary: For twenty-two years, since a fateful baseball game against their rival town, it has rained in Moundville, so when the rain finally stops, twelve-year-old Roy, his friends, and foster brother Sturgis dare to face the curse and form a team.
ISBN 978-0-375-85579-5 (trade) — ISBN 978-0-375-95579-2 (lib. bdg.)
— ISBN 978-0-375-89156-4 (e-book)
[1. Baseball—Fiction. 2. Foster home care—Fiction. 3. Rain and rainfall—Fiction.
4. Family life—Minnesota—Fiction. 5. Blessing and cursing—Fiction. 6. Dakota Indians—Fiction.
7. Indians of North America—Minnesota—Fiction. 8. Minnesota—Fiction.] I. Title.
PZ7.S27912Mud 2009
[Fic]—dc22
2008000166

ISBN 978-0-375-84472-0 (pbk.)

Printed in the United States of America
10 9 8 7 6 5 4 3
First Yearling Edition

For Ken and Kelly,
with whom I learned the heights of friendship
and rivalry known only among brothers.

A father makes all the difference.

—Roy Hobbs in *The Natural*

Prologue

My father says the defining moment of his life came when he was twelve years old.

"The defining moment in a person's life isn't necessarily the greatest moment," he tells me. "When you were born, Roy, that was the *greatest* moment in my life. But this was the *defining* moment. It's the moment everybody knows me by. It's the moment I knew exactly who I was."

"Who's that?"

"The luckiest son of a gun there ever was, that's who."

This moment came on the Fourth of July, during the last baseball game he ever played. It was the annual game between our hometown of Moundville and our archrival, Sinister Bend. It was the bottom of the fourth inning, and Moundville was trailing by eleven runs.

It was nothing new for Moundville to be losing—they had lost over a hundred straight games to Sinister Bend, as far back as they'd been writing down the score and keeping track. It was unusual to be losing by that much, though, and that early in the game. Especially because it was supposed to be different that year: Moundville had a young player named Bobby Fitz, a boy who could throw a spitball without using spit and smack singles all over the field and stretch them into doubles and steal third while he was at it. Bobby Fitz was expected to lead Moundville to victory. It wasn't just his pitching, or even his hitting. There was something invulnerable about him, something glowing and magical. Something that didn't care about curses or losing streaks or anything but winning.

Bobby got hurt in the first inning and came out of the game. Moundville's backup pitcher struggled, giving up a run or two for every hard-earned out. The fans covered their eyes with each pitch.

Things weren't any better when Moundville batted. The Sinister Bend pitcher was a monster. The batters could barely see his eyes scowling from underneath a mop of long, dark hair, though they could see his mouth twisted into a permanent sneer. He threw every ball as if he was trying to puncture a hole in the backstop. The Moundville players were terrified. They jumped back half the time just to watch fastballs bisect the plate.

Seeing black clouds creep in across the sky, the Moundville coach corralled the boys in the dugout and told them to take their time. Hold up the game, he said. Pray for rain. By long-standing rule, the game wouldn't be official until the fourth inning was done. If they could just prolong the inning until the sky opened up, Moundville could reschedule the game in a week or so, when their star pitcher was healthy again.

The first batter dawdled all he could but lasted only a few minutes. The second flailed at the first pitch and grounded out.

My father was Moundville's last hope. He stood in the batter's box for nearly half an hour, fouling off pitches,

4

stamping around in the dirt, and adjusting his gloves between every pitch, until the Sinister Bend pitcher looked ready to take off his head with a fastball.

His defining moment came on the thirty-second pitch. By that time, the sky had opened, sending sheets of rain across the baseball field while lightning was flashing in the distance.

The hit itself was nothing—a lucky seeing-eye single that squirted on wet grass by the diving third baseman and skittered to the fence. It was booted and mishandled and overthrown by the defense, mostly due to the slippery conditions. My dad even came around to score, on a single and three bases' worth of errors by the Sinister Bend team.

It didn't make much of a dent in the box score. It made all the difference, though, because the game was called just one out short of being official. All eleven Sinister Bend runs were off the books. If it wasn't for the rain and lightning, the Moundville players might have carried my dad off the field on their shoulders. Instead, they huddled in the dugout, waiting for the storm to blow over.

The spectators all ran to the diner and the pool hall and the pizza place, which were across the street, packing every building right up to the rafters. My dad said you could see the sides of those buildings bulge like overcooked wieners, but he tends to stretch the truth. People crowded together at the windows and watched the sky and wondered when it would let up enough to leave. It just kept pouring, though, so people started running to their cars—or running home, if they'd walked to the park that morning. They ran in wet little groups of three and four, hardly able to see where they were going.

Meanwhile, the Sinister Bend team refused to yield. They sat in their dugout, looking with determined eyes at the Moundville team, who also refused to yield. If the Sinister Bend team would wait, so would they. The dugouts were covered, but sheets of rain were sweeping in, keeping the boys plenty wet and miserable.

"It was a game of wet chicken," my dad likes to say.

It grew dark, and the parents of boys on both sides began to drive by, flashing their lights in the mist and honking their horns. Every time a car passed, one or two boys would have to quit the standoff and go home.

The last two boys were my father and the Sinister Bend pitcher. They were the only ones whose parents had not come to pick them up and take them home. They waited, wet and cold, in different corners of the muddy diamond, a full hour after every single other person had gone home.

At last, the Sinister Bend pitcher stood up and stepped out of the rain. He did not turn and run, though. He stormed to the Moundville dugout and rattled the chain-link fencing that protected the players from hard-hit foul balls.

"This isn't over!" he shouted at my dad. "Not by a long shot!"

It still isn't over, twenty-two years later. After all, it's still raining.

Chapter 1

To understand baseball, you have to understand percentages. For example, if a guy is hitting .250, he only has about one chance in a thousand of going five-for-five in a single game. Over a season, though, the odds get better. Like about one in seven. Not great, but not that bad. If he plays long enough, he'll probably do it. That's how a guy can go into every game feeling positive. He knows if he plays enough games, eventually he'll have a perfect day at the plate.

It's the same thing with rain. Maybe you read in the paper every day that there's a 25 percent chance of rain. That means there's about one chance in a thousand of having it rain five days straight. It's not likely, but it's not impossible. If you're twelve years old, like I am, you've probably even seen it happen.

If you take all the teams in the history of baseball, then percentages start making funny things happen. For example, Walt Dropo of Detroit once got twelve hits in a row; he went five-for-five one day and seven-for-seven the next. The odds of that are like one in two million, but there's been way more than two million tries, if you think about all the baseball players and all the games they ever played in, so it had to happen eventually. Dropo was just the guy who did it.

That's how I explain the fact that it's been raining for twenty-two years in Moundville. The earth is a big place, and it's been around for a long time. If you think about all the towns in the world and all the years the earth has been around, it was bound to happen somewhere sooner or later. It just happened to be my town and my lifetime. It's percentages.

I'm trying to explain this to Adam on the last day of baseball camp while we're packing up to go home. Camp is at the state university, and we've been sharing a dorm room about the size of a breadbox.

"Everybody's hitting .250?" he asks me. "Even the DH?"

"For the sake of argument, yeah."

"Sounds like a pretty lousy baseball team." He shakes his head. "The manager would send some guys down or something. Maybe make a trade."

"That's not the point."

"It is so the point! If your whole team is batting .250, you don't wait around until the end of time because maybe eventually a guy goes five-for-five. You do something about it."

"We can't do anything about the weather, though."

"You can move."

"It's not that easy. My dad's business is in Moundville."

"He can start a business somewhere else."

"He rainproofs houses," I remind him. "It's not like there's a big demand for that anywhere else."

"I would move anyway," he says. "No baseball? That's nuts."

"It's not such a bad place to live. Anyway, there's lots of places where it rains all the time. London. Seattle."

"It doesn't rain every day for twenty-two years straight."

"It could, though."

"Whatever."

I like Adam pretty well, but I'm kind of mad at him for dumping on Moundville. Sure, it's wet, but it's still my hometown.

Fortunately, we're interrupted by a half dozen people practically knocking down the door. It's Steve and his family.

Steve is also from Moundville. We've known each other since kindergarten. His parents and his little sisters and his grandma came down to watch the Camp Classic, and now they're all heading home.

The Camp Classic is a four-team tournament meant to end camp with a bang. Adam and I were on the winning team. He pitched the first game, and I caught both games. My shins still feel like they're about to fall off at the knees, but it was worth it.

"You're coming with us!" says one of Steve's sisters. It must be Shauna because she's wearing a red T-shirt. They color-code the twins so everyone can tell them apart.

"Your dad can't make it!" the other sister, Sheila, explains.

"Shush," says their dad. "Let the man talk to his father." He passes me a cell phone.

"Yeah?" I shout into the phone.

"Hey, kid. No need to yell." My dad's voice is as clear as if he's standing right next to me, a testament to Mr. Robinson's commitment to high-end gadgetry. "I hear you won a trophy?"

"It's nothing." I figure Steve's dad must have told him about my Camp Classic MVP trophy.

"It didn't sound like nothing."

"Those trophies are like immunizations. Everybody has to get one." It's true, too. Adam won a trophy for "best competitor," which meant he took the game too seriously, and Steve won one for "best sport," which meant he didn't take the game seriously enough.

"Anyway," he says, "I got tied up with some stuff here in Moundville, so I asked Steve's dad to give you a lift back."

"Sure. What's going on?" Usually it means someone's rainproof house is leaking and my dad has to go and fix it. He gives out a five-year warranty that's no end of grief.

"It's kind of a surprise. You'll find out when you get home. See you soon!" He hangs up on me, and I hand the phone back to Mr. Robinson.

"Thanks for giving me a ride."

"We're happy to have you along. Maybe the girls will bug you instead of bugging the rest of us." Mr. Robinson thinks this is hilarious, and so do Steve's mom and grandma. "Anyway, we're parked right outside. See you in a bit."

We can hear the twins racing to the end of the hall and their mom begging them to slow down before the door swings shut behind them.

⚘ ⚘ ⚘

"So I guess I'll see you when we're in the big leagues?" Adam asks as we leave the dorm for the last time.

"Sure thing. Get drafted by the same team, okay? I don't want to hit your stuff."

Adam is the only kid I know with a legitimate curveball. I've seen him carve up batters like they were turkeys with that thing. He's small, though. You don't see too many pint-sized pitchers in the majors. So who knows if he'll make it to the bigs?

We trade a clumsy hug, and that's that.

The drive is about two hours, but it's going to be a long couple of hours. For one thing, Mr. Robinson is always trying to help us appreciate the contributions of African Americans to American music, and his lesson this car trip is on the most inaccessible jazz music ever recorded. I like Louis Armstrong, but John Coltrane sounds like a snare drum beating up a saxophone.

For another thing, I have to sit between the twins, and they have a little contest to see who can ask me the most questions the fastest.

"What's your favorite baseball team?" Sheila asks.

"I don't know. The Tigers, maybe."

"Why the Tigers?" Shauna asks.

"Because Pudge plays for them."

"Who's Pudge?" Sheila asks.

"Ivan Rodriguez."

"Is he your favorite player?" Shauna asks.

"Kind of, yeah."

"Why?" Sheila asks. I feel like I'm watching a tennis match.

"Because he's a really good catcher and I'm a catcher."

"Is he cute?" This sets off a giggle bomb, and it's a while before they settle down.

"So are you going to play catcher?" Shauna asks.

"I already do."

"I mean, when you grow up?"

"You never know," I tell her.

"Why don't you know?"

"It's a tough job to get," I tell her. "There are millions of kids who want to play baseball, but there are only thirty starting catchers in Major League Baseball."

"Only thirty?"

"Exactly thirty."

"How do you know?"

"Because there are thirty teams, silly."

"Name them!" says Sheila.

I sigh and start to rattle off names while the girls count on their hands. They also make me name the catcher for each team and tell them whether or not he's cute. They also think I've named one twice, and I have to explain that there's more than one Molina and they're brothers, but the girls think I'm making it up because I made a mistake, so we're halfway to Moundville before I can take a breath.

❦ ❦ ❦

We live in a very flat state, so you can see Moundville from far away, a big bump on the prairie. When it comes into view, with the familiar gray haze of clouds over it, I feel a little twist in my stomach that's part dread and part homesickness.

"Daddy, rest stop, one mile!" Sheila hollers, pointing at a blue sign. Mr. Robinson nods and puts on the blinker.

I don't need to use the facilities myself, but I do want to stretch my legs one more time in dry outside air, so I walk around a little bit.

It seems like all the rest stops around here have historic significance. For example, this one has a plaque about a skirmish during the Sioux Uprising, which makes for interesting reading. The sign says that twelve people died on both sides of the battle. I wonder how the deceased would feel about the site being memorialized with public toilets.

"Pretty sordid stuff," says Mr. Robinson, who sees me reading the plaque. He reads it himself and clucks. "It should say 'Dakota War.' Nobody calls it the Sioux Uprising anymore. Both words are inaccurate." I just nod, hoping he won't start lecturing me. Mr. Robinson is a history teacher and will talk as long as you let him.

Sure enough, though, once we're back in the car, he goes into teacher mode.

"People don't want to think about it too much, but this area has some ugly history. Brutal conflicts between the white settlers and the natives. It started when the U.S.

government didn't make good on some supplies they promised. People were starving, and the store owners on the reservation wouldn't give food on credit. To add insult to injury, one store owner said—"

"Dad," Sheila whines, "this isn't history class."

"It's interesting, is all." Mr. Robinson lapses into thoughtful silence, looking back and forth across the road, maybe seeing the ghosts of the past playing out their endless battles.

There used to be a Native American trading post where Sinister Bend is now, and the traders got along pretty well with the settlers. The trading post mostly dealt in furs, which was a wintertime business. The traders' kids didn't have as much to do in the summer. They saw the settlers' kids playing baseball and asked if they could play, too. That was where the whole rivalry began—especially when the natives started beating the settlers at their own game. Eventually, the trading post turned into Sinister Bend, and the pioneer settlement turned into Moundville.

According to local stories, one of the soldiers sent to protect the trading post learned the game directly from Abner Doubleday at Fort Sumter and was transferred up here a few weeks before the Civil War started. I don't believe that any more than I believe that Doubleday invented baseball. Still, I wish I could see those old games, which were played with bats the players carved themselves and a ball made out of horsehide wrapped around sawdust—one that wouldn't go a hundred feet if Barry Bonds gave it his best rip.

I'm not that much into history, except when it comes to baseball.

Both of the twins have fallen asleep on me, so I can barely move, and my left arm is asleep. I know we're nearly home, though, because the rain picks up, spattering the windshield of the SUV. Sure enough, a moment later the famous sign flashes by, reading "Welcome to Moundville," with the letters *o* and *n* crossed out. The town has tried every kind of plastic cover and paintproof coating, but vandals always find a way to cross out those two letters.

Steve groans and pulls the brim of his cap over his eyes. I know just how he feels.

Chapter 2

Well, Mudville is a good name for it. Twenty-two years of rain have destroyed the grass and killed all the trees. Most of the topsoil has been washed away, exposing the gray clay underneath. I suppose, given enough time, the muddy clay will wash away, too, and Moundville will be left clinging to a pile of granite.

There's less joy in our Mudville than the one in the poem. Maybe mighty Casey struck out, but at least those guys got to watch a baseball game.

We pull into the driveway of my house, a long rambler with sheets of heavy-duty plastic arced over the roof like the protective wings of a mother bird. That's my dad's rainproofing. Most of the houses in Moundville have it, and the ones that don't aren't suited for living in. From the air, Moundville probably looks like so many misshapen igloos on a bank of filthy snow.

We all say "Goodbye" and "Thanks" and "See you soon," and eventually I grab my bags and climb over Shauna and out of the car. I hustle up the walk like it's a base path but still get pretty drenched.

"I'm home!" I drop my bags by the door and use my hand to squeegee the water off my head. Then I step out of the foyer into the living room and stop dead in my tracks.

There's a kid about my own age stretched out on the couch, watching television. He's wearing a flannel shirt and corduroy pants, even though it's over eighty degrees out. One of his loafers is held together with duct tape. He's tanner than anyone I've ever seen, and his hair hasn't been cut in a long time.

So there's my dad's surprise, I think. I don't know what it means, though. Maybe some homeless people he knows are visiting from out of town?

"Still raining?" the boy asks, seeing how wet I am.

When I get a better look at him, I see his face is a mess of scar tissue on the right side. His ear is unnaturally pink, and I realize it's a fake one.

"It's been raining for over twenty years," I tell him. "It never stops."

"I know. I was kind of kidding." So he's a comedian, too. I should ask him who's on first.

"I'm Roy," I tell him. "I live here."

"Hey. I'm Sturgis. I live here, too. As of about"—he looks at the clock on the cable box—"two and a half hours ago."

"Huh?"

"I'm like a foster kid. Your dad didn't tell you about me?"

"Nah, but it's good," I say, as though I'm used to coming home and finding the living room strewn about with new siblings. "Where are you from?"

"Between here and Sutton," he says, which is funny. I don't think there *is* anything between here and Sutton.

"So where's my dad?"

"In the kitchen making dinner."

17

I shudder and know I'll miss the excellent camp food I've gotten used to.

The kitchen looks like a small tornado has tried to make a spaghetti omelet. There's something boiling on the stove, and the counter is cluttered with open cans and dripping bowls. Our old orange Manx cat, Yogi, is licking a broken egg on the floor. He's a weird cat. We've had him since before I was born. He's probably about 112 in cat years.

"Roy!" My dad gives me an awkward hug and gets something sticky on my shirt. "Sorry I didn't hear you come in," he says. "Hey, can you please get me the Dijon mustard and Tabasco?"

I nudge Yogi aside to get the condiments out of the fridge while my father adds big chunks of Spam to the blender and pushes a button.

"Did you meet Sturgis?" He spoons mustard and Tabasco into the mixture and gives the blender another spin. "He's only two months older than you, you know. You guys are practically twins."

"Yeah, I met him."

"Great. Hey, can you put those noodles in a baking dish?"

"So what's the story with him anyway?"

"The noodles, Roy! They're overcooking!"

I pour the boiling contents of the pot into a colander to drain. When the steam clears, I see that it's manicotti tubes. I peel them apart and lay them out in the baking dish.

"So what's going on?" I ask again.

"Well, his mom passed away, and his dad . . . Well, you know about some kids' dads, right?"

"Sure."

"Darn it, I was supposed to put tomato sauce on this." My dad looks forlornly at his Spam manicotti. I hope he tosses the whole mess and sends out for a pizza instead. "Well, I'll put tomato soup on it. That'll be just as good." He grabs a jar of Campbell's from the cupboard and dumps it over the manicotti.

"Anyway, Sturgis was living with his grandma, but they decided she couldn't take care of him anymore. She could barely take care of herself anymore. Serious health problems. So now he's living with us."

"But when—when did you do all this? Like, sign up to be a foster dad?"

"I didn't really mean to," he explains. "I just asked about it, thinking . . . I don't know, that I could get information and see if we qualified, then you'd come back and we'd talk about it and see where it went."

"So why didn't you?"

"I think once they have your name, you're in some kind of database. Like, if they have more kids than they have places, they go to that database and start making calls. Sturgis, he was an emergency situation. One more kid than they had any room for. So they called me out of the blue and asked me if I could do it for the time being."

"They didn't have *anywhere* else for him to go?"

"Apparently not."

"So what would happen if you said no? Would he go to a homeless shelter? Or would he sleep on a cot in someone's office until they found a place for him?"

"I don't know," my dad admits. "Just drop it, okay? He is staying with us, so it doesn't matter."

"I was just wondering." What does happen to kids nobody wants? I don't think there are orphanages anymore. "Do you know what happened to him? His ear and everything?"

"It's a lucky kid who makes it through life whole. Hey, maybe you can get Sturgis settled a bit before dinner? We'll eat in about half an hour."

"Sure," I tell him. "Um . . . where's he going to sleep?"

"I thought your room?" He's looking at me closely, to see how I'll react. The fact is, I like having my own room, even if it's big enough for two. I don't really want to share. It's hard to hold it against a kid who's an emergency situation, though.

"I'm just not ready to give up the home office," my dad explains. "It's my only office."

"It's okay," I tell him, acting like it's no big deal. "I have to go unpack anyway. I'll carve out a space for him among the stuff."

"You're a great kid, Roy." He puts the pan in the oven and prepares to do something with a bag of frozen spinach and a can of mandarin oranges.

"Darn it," he says, looking in the fridge, "I'm out of

Miracle Whip. Now how am I supposed to make the spinach salad?"

I dump my clothes from camp into the hamper, then open the bottom dresser drawer, which is all sweaters and stuff, and pack them into the suitcase. I don't know what I'll do come winter if he's still here, but it'll do for now. I also clear out a shelf on the bookcase, just by moving things around. I have an extra bed in my room that buddies use when they stay over, so at least that's not a problem. Until one of my buddies wants to stay over, that is.

I go into the living room when I'm done. Sturgis is still sprawled out on the couch, and Yogi is sprawled out on Sturgis, gingerly rubbing his nose on Sturgis's chin.

"What happened to his tail?" Sturgis wants to know. Everybody asks that. Yogi doesn't have much of a tail—just a fuzzy little bump. Manx tails are just like that, but people who don't know much about cats think he met with an accident.

"It's a lucky cat who makes it through life whole." I usually tell company all about Manx cats when they ask, but maybe Sturgis will feel better thinking he's not the only one with a missing part.

"He's nice. I never had a cat before." He smiles at Yogi and scratches his cheeks until Yogi is all squinty-eyed and blissful.

"So you want to unpack?"

"Okay." He gently nudges Yogi aside and gets up. I realize he's taller than me. I'm kind of tall myself, but Sturgis towers over me. It's because he has freakishly long legs, I think. He grabs a couple of department store bags from the corner. For a second, I think he's brought us presents, but then I see they're full of old clothes and stuff. Those paper bags are his luggage.

"You can put your clothes in the bottom drawer," I tell him as we go into the bedroom. "Let me know if you need another drawer. I can probably clear one out." I probably can't, but I want to show off what a good host I am.

"I'm good for now." He shoves the bags back into a corner by his bed.

"I cleared off a shelf, too."

"All right. Hey, what's all this?" He walks over to my side of the room and pokes at my trophies a bit. "Are you a star jock or something?"

"I play baseball. They give out a lot of trophies." I wish he wouldn't touch them, but I don't say anything.

"How do you play baseball if it rains all the time?"

"My buddy Steve and I used to play in Sutton Little League."

"You don't play anymore?"

"Not in Sutton. Steve decided it was too much work, and his dad was my ride."

"You don't have room for any more trophies anyway," he snorts.

"Do you play?"

22

"Nah, not really." He seems fascinated by the trophies, though, touching them and reading the engravings until my father calls us in to dinner.

I think of my father's cooking the same way I think of rain and school. I have to live with it, but I don't have to like it. The Spam manicotti does nothing to change my mind. Sturgis gobbles it right up, though. What's worse, he forks the whole mess into a mush and mixes it with the spinach, eating it with four or five slices of garlic bread and washing it all down with about a quart of milk.

"You like that, eh, Stuey?" my dad asks.

"It's okay," Sturgis says through a mouthful of food. I figure he just hasn't had a meal in about two months.

"So . . ." My dad rubs his hands expectantly. "Are you going to tell us about baseball camp? Did I hear something about a trophy?"

"You know, they give out a lot of trophies." I really don't want to come off as a bragger, especially in front of Sturgis. I don't even know if I like him yet, but I do want him to like me.

The three of us lapse into a silence, and I wonder if anyone will tell me the whole story about how Sturgis got hurt, and how he became an emergency situation, and what happened to his parents, and why he doesn't have anybody else to take him in, and exactly how it became my problem. There's just the clattering of forks on plates, though.

"I don't know what I'm going to do the rest of the summer," I say instead. "Maybe play summer basketball? Do you play, Sturge?" I figure, with his height, he could be a natural.

"Sturgis," he corrects me. It's pretty formal for a guy who's crashing in my bedroom and uses paper bags for luggage. "I don't play basketball," he adds.

"Well," says my dad, "I thought maybe you two could come to work with me anyway. I could use some help."

"Will we go up on the roofs?" I ask. Guys have to crawl around on high, wet, angled rooftops, assembling the frame of the rainproof sheeting, then attaching the sheeting to the frame. I think it would be pretty cool to do that kind of work.

"We can't have you on the roof," my dad says. "It's too dangerous. A strong wind can pick up a sheet of plastic and carry it off like a kite, and a grown man with it. I've seen it happen."

I've heard that story before. I used to imagine that man, doomed to sail high above the earth, shivering from the cold, lonely and hungry, clinging to the plastic sheet as if it was a magic carpet. Now I think my dad is making it up.

Sturgis believes it, though. He's staring at him with his mouth agape. "I'll go up there if you want," he says at last. "I'm a good climber."

"You'll be digging ditches for now—and I mean digging the old-fashioned way."

My dad once bought a machine to do it, but the muddy conditions made it hard to drive the thing. It was always

24

getting stuck, and drivers were always crashing into fences and the sides of houses. So they went back to shovels and wheelbarrows.

"Maybe over time you can work your way up, though," he adds.

"Work my way up!" Sturgis laughs and slaps the table. "Good one." It's kind of a fake laugh, and I guess that he's trying to get in good with his new family. My dad just beams, though. He's found the perfect son: someone who likes his cooking and laughs at his jokes.

"I'll clean up. You guys take it easy," my dad offers after dinner, which is weird because usually I have to clean up.

"By the way, Roy!" he shouts from the kitchen. "You have mail on the end table by the couch!"

I go to the living room and find it. There's three issues of *Sports Illustrated*, one letter from St. James Academy, and a postcard from my mom. I sit down on the sofa to read the postcard and the letter. Yogi wanders over from the far side of the couch to sit in my lap.

"Hey, buddy," says Sturgis, coming into the room to sit on the other side of the sofa. He's talking to Yogi, not me. The cat goes back over and lets Sturgis pet him, sticking his butt up in the air the way he does when he's happy.

The postcard is from Victory Field in Indianapolis. My mom is a flight attendant and never passes through a city with a baseball park without sending me a postcard.

"Had a day off in Indy. It was raining, so I didn't see any

baseball," she's written on the back. "There's a zoo next door, and I saw giraffes. They are beautiful animals. Love, Mom."

"Giraffes are beautiful animals," I tell Sturgis by way of conversation.

"Giraffes are all right."

The letter is from the admissions guy at St. James Academy, in Sutton. I scan it quickly.

"St. James needs to know if I'm going!" I shout to my dad.

"I know!" he hollers back, over the crash and clanging of washing dishes.

"It's this school in Sutton," I tell Sturgis.

"I know. I've heard of it."

"I'm supposed to go next year." The Moundville school only goes through sixth grade. We're not even big enough anymore for a junior high school, let alone a senior high school.

"You'll have to wear a uniform."

"Yeah, but they have great athletics. Their baseball team is one of the best in the state. It would be really good for me."

"Hey," he says, looking up.

My dad brings in a lopsided cake and sets it on the coffee table. He tried to put on the chocolate frosting while the cake was still hot, so it's half melted into a glaze.

"I don't know how to do letters in frosting, so you have to pretend it says 'Welcome Home, Roy and Sturgis.'"

The cake is about as soft and moist as a hockey puck. I put a little mound of ice cream on my piece to soften it.

"So, Sturgis," my dad says, "do you want to tell Roy more about yourself?"

Sturgis gives me a long, careful look. He's chewing his cake, and it takes him a while to finish chewing.

"I'm a foster kid. You've probably seen TV movies about us."

"I don't know. Maybe one or two."

"Well, there you go." He goes off down the hall to use the bathroom.

"Hey, does Mom know about Sturgis?" I ask my dad. Since he's never technically divorced my mom, I wonder what she'd say, coming home and finding a whole new kid hanging around. Sure, she's been gone for four years—nearly five years, actually. Still, shouldn't she have a say? Now she's abandoned a whole nother kid she doesn't even know about.

My dad looks kind of thoughtful, trying to figure out how to answer. "Sturgis is my, uh, my project," he says at last. "Do you want some more cake?"

Chapter 3

I head to bed after *Sunday Night Baseball* and find Sturgis crashed on his bed, listening to his tape player and looking at one of my dad's books on landscaping. Yogi has knocked over one of his brown paper suitcases and is now nested in a pile of laundry.

"You actually have a Walkman? Most everyone I know has an iPod or at least a CD player."

"Huh?" He lifts the headphone over his good ear.

"Just saying the Astros beat the White Sox." On second thought, the whole bit about iPods sounds obnoxious.

"Good for them." He turns off the player. "There's nothing in here about the stuff we're going to be doing." He tosses the book on the nightstand with a resounding *whomp*.

"That's because my dad invented it."

"No kidding?"

I tell him the whole story: A year or so after it started raining, my dad realized there was a profit in it. At first, it was an odd job, like mowing lawns. He went door to door, offering to cover people's roofs with plastic. He'd just lay it out flat and tie the corners to the eaves. A few customers lost shingles and drainpipes when strong winds pulled on the sheets, though, so my dad read engineering books and did experiments at home and came up with a better way of doing things. So was born the Rain Redirection System. He got a patent for it and everything.

"Wow. Are you guys rich?" Sturgis asks.

"There's not many places that need that much protection from rain. He does okay, though."

"Yeah." He looks around, maybe thinking about our house and stuff. Maybe, compared to him, we are rich.

He gets up and strips down to his undies. Before he flicks off the light and gets into bed, I see more scars along his right side, from his shoulder down to his thigh.

"My dad used to be a professional baseball player," he says suddenly.

"Really?" I wonder if he's making it up. "So are you guys rich?" I don't see how he could be, but you never know.

"That was a long time ago and not for very long," he explains.

I'm curious to know more, but he's already asleep, snoring along with the familiar rhythm of rain splashing down on the plastic-covered roof.

We go to the work site bright and early the next morning. Okay, it's not exactly bright—just early. Sturgis and I are both wearing the candy-apple-red raincoats everyone wears when they work for my dad. They have his company logo on the back, silk-screened in gold.

My dad's the only one with an umbrella instead of a raincoat. Then again, my dad's the only one wearing a suit. He drives around a lot, meeting customers and suppliers and so on. If he wore a raincoat, those people wouldn't even know that he was wearing a suit.

"Who lives here?" Sturgis wonders, looking up at the house in awe. It's more like a mansion, but it's pretty run-down.

"Nobody lives here. It's being flipped," my dad explains. It's what my dad calls a derelict home—one that was abandoned by its owners in the rain. Lately, some real estate guys have been buying up the derelict houses, fixing them up, and selling them. More and more people from Sutton are buying houses here because they're relatively cheap.

This one is big enough to be a bed-and-breakfast or something. It's shaped a bit like a V, with the wide part in front and gables and dormers and whatnot sticking out everywhere. There's even a portico in front with columns, but it's half crumbled, looking like some Greek ruin.

"Remember to call me sir, and no back talk," my dad says as we walk around to the back. "I have to keep up my image."

"Yes, sir," says Sturgis while I swallow a smart reply.

"This is Frank," my dad tells Sturgis when we find him. "He'll be your boss."

Frank is one of my dad's oldest buddies, so I know him pretty well. He's a big guy, looks like he could be the entire linebacker corps for the Chicago Bears, but he's nice when you get to know him. He's sipping a big thermos of coffee and shouting orders at a couple of guys setting up a makeshift tent. The tent gives us workers a place to get out of the rain for lunch and coffee breaks.

"Frank, I've got a couple of strong young backs for you,"

my dad says. "You know Roy. The other one here is Sturgis. Don't treat them any different than anyone else."

"Of course not," says Frank. Since my dad sometimes gripes that Frank isn't tough enough on his crew, I'm not too worried. "Hey, Roy. Hey, Sturgis."

"Hey, Frank," I say.

"Good morning, mister," says Sturgis.

"You guys do what he says," my dad tells us.

"Yes, sir," we both say.

My dad looks at his watch. "Darn it, I'm already running late," he says, and runs off to the car, juggling his car keys and the umbrella.

"You guys are in for a real fun day," says Frank. "We have about an acre here, and we need new ditches across two sides of it. Both of you, grab a barrow."

There are a couple of ugly little wheelbarrows standing by. We each take one, and Frank picks up a couple of shovels. We follow him, pushing the wobbly wheelbarrows across the expanse of gray matter that people in Moundville call a yard, for lack of a better word.

Every street in Moundville has a little canal, about eight inches wide, on one side or the other. The streets slant a bit, so the water drains into the canal, then sluices out of town. Every property has to have drainage, too—ditches to move all the water that falls on the house and yard into the street canal. In this case, the ditch is so clogged up with mud it's barely any good.

31

"We also have to fill in the old ditch," Frank tells us. "Have you ever dug clay?"

"Not much, no."

"It's heavy." He scans the property and points out a spot. "We'll start digging there. Do you know why?"

I shrug and mumble something about it being as good a place as any.

"So our moat won't fill up with water," Sturgis guesses. "We start at the low point and dig backward, so the moat drains as we go."

"Smart kid." Frank plants the shovels in the mud. "You guys try not to get in each other's way. When you fill your barrow, go dump it on the pile." He points vaguely at the far corner of the property. "That's the pile." He pats our backs like a friendly giant and returns to supervise the raising of the tent.

"It's a drainage ditch," I tell Sturgis. "Not a moat. There's no crocodiles in it."

"Whatever."

We grab our shovels and get to work. I start closer to the canal, with Sturgis a few feet in front.

The other guys are setting up the ropes and weights to keep one another from falling off the roof or getting carried away by a strong wind. If anyone really was carried off, I bet it was a long time ago. They're pretty careful now, it looks like.

After about an hour of shoveling, I've barely made a dent in the ground, and my shoulders are already sore. Sturgis is doing much better. His wheelbarrow is nearly full.

I look at my watch. "Do you want to take a break? Dad said we get one short break in the morning."

"You go ahead." He tosses a scoop of mud into the barrow.

If I can't talk to someone, a break is just standing around in the rain. So I keep working, counting shovelfuls.

I try again after another hundred scoops of mud. "We should really take our break now. Otherwise, we'll miss it. It'll be lunch soon."

"You go ahead." Sturgis plants his shovel into the mud before setting off to dump the barrow on the pile.

I can't understand how he is so far ahead of me. It's not that he's stronger, I think. He's just faster. I wonder if maybe the ground is softer where Sturgis is or if he has a better shovel. I grab his shovel and dig up some mud. It's the same kind of mud and the same kind of shovel.

Frank comes up behind me. He whistles and slaps me on the back. "Good work. Come on, junior, we're taking an early lunch." It doesn't surprise me he's already hungry. I'm hungry myself now that he mentions it.

Frank sees Sturgis returning with his wheelbarrow. "Leave the barrow, kid. It's lunchtime."

"You guys go ahead." Sturgis picks up his shovel.

"You got to take a break," says Frank. "It's the law."

Sturgis reluctantly plants his shovel.

Frank elbows me in the ribs and whispers, "He just feels bad because you're so far ahead."

I try to tell Frank the truth, but he's gone, hollering to

everyone that it's lunchtime. He finally sends some guy off to get burgers, and I have a chance to talk to him.

"Sturgis dug the big hole," I tell him. "He's been working really hard."

"You're a good kid, Roy." He claps me on the back. "You can work for me anytime." He goes back to joking around with his buddies. I feel a little bit better.

"Hey, you're the McGuire kid, right?" a fellow wants to know when I sit down. I don't really know the guy. I think his name is Ted or Tom or something. He's one of the youngest guys on the crew, like maybe he just got out of high school. Or dropped out, even.

"That's me."

"And who's the funny-looking kid? The one you were working with?"

"He's my new foster brother."

"Your dad takes in strays?"

"I guess so."

I realize Sturgis has come to join us, but he veers away and leaves the tent.

"He's a good guy," I tell Tom or Ted, feeling a little guilty.

The burgers come, but the bags go all the way through the line before they come to me. I get the last two burgers and one box of fries. Sturgis and I will have to share, I suppose.

I don't see him anywhere, though. I poke my head out of the tent but don't see him. I walk around the building and glance up at a ladder just in time to see one duct-taped shoe disappearing over the top.

34

I climb one-handed up the ladder, holding the bag of food. It's not easy. When I finally reach the top, Sturgis is sitting in a small cave of plastic where the workers have begun building the Rain Redirection System.

"Are you going to have lunch?" I push the bag at him.

"Sure." He reaches into the bag for a (slightly wet, mostly cold) hamburger.

"That guy I was talking to is just some idiot."

"Oh, heck, I've heard a lot worse." He unwraps his burger.

"I told Frank you did all the work, too. He just made a mistake. So if you're mad about that . . ."

"It's no big deal. Frank doesn't really care if we do anything anyway."

"What do you mean?"

"We're just some kids his boss foisted on him. He doesn't care how much work we do. He just wants us to stay out of the way."

"I don't know. Dad says they're shorthanded."

"Maybe they are, but we're just kids. We're not that much help." He's already done with his burger. I get my own while I can. I must be pretty hungry, because even cold, it's not bad.

"So why do you work so hard?"

"I don't know. To show you up?"

I laugh. "You're doing a good job."

"Wow, check that out."

I turn around. Through a flap in the plastic, we can see

down the hill, past Moundville, to a swampy wasteland of crumbling, abandoned houses and buildings, descending into a massive lake. You can still see the peak of a church, poking above the water about two hundred feet from shore.

"That's Sinister Bend," I tell him. "What's left of it anyway."

"I know. It's just amazing to see it from up here."

When the rain began, it filled the streets and fields with water, then found the crest of the hill and sluiced down the south side of the mound into the Narrows River. The river backed up and overflowed, filling the town of Sinister Bend like a cereal bowl. Everyone here has seen the footage: water up to the roofs of the houses, and sometimes people on the roofs calling for help and waving their hands in desperation as the water came up around their legs. Even after the Army Engineers built the canals, Sinister Bend was mostly underwater. The whole town was just washed off the face of the earth.

Sturgis has finished the fries and is now peering into the bag, as if another hamburger or maybe a milk shake is hiding in the corner.

"Well," he says as he stuffs the lunch bag into his back pocket, "guess it's back to the salt mine."

"I think we have more break time coming to us," I say, but he's already clambering across the roof and down the ladder, as nimble as a squirrel. I finish my burger alone, then descend to the muddy doom of an afternoon's work.

Chapter 4

"So how was your first day of work?" my dad wants to know when he picks us up.

"Kind of boring," I say honestly.

"It was okay," says Sturgis.

"It could have been worse," I add, but if there are worse jobs than digging mud in the rain for nine or ten hours, I don't even want to know what they are. I just don't want to be the whiner while Sturgis acts tough.

I kill time before dinner checking my e-mail. Besides all the spam and junk that collected while I was away, I have one message from Steve and one from Adam. Steve asks if I can play basketball tomorrow, so I write about this job I'm suddenly stuck doing. I go on a bit about how lousy it is, then delete most of it. Steve doesn't need to read all that. Instead, I just say that I'm helping out my dad all week but we can play basketball on the weekend.

Adam writes that he's going to a pro game in Kansas City and he gets to meet some of the players because of this deal they have for up-and-coming baseball players. Do I want any autographs? I rack my brain and can't think of anyone, so I tell him to surprise me.

It occurs to me after I send off the e-mails that I didn't tell either one of them about my new foster brother. I wonder if that's weird.

Dinner is fish stick casserole. It's not any better than it sounds. Sturgis puts away two or three plates while I labor over the first. He asks my dad about the details of the Rain Redirection System. My dad is only too happy to talk about the venting that keeps the plastic from inflating and the convex pleats that keep the plastic from filling up with water. Sturgis nods and takes it all in. It's pretty boring to me, but I already know a lot more about those things than I care to. Between the food and the conversation, it's a wonder I make it through dinner without going facedown in a pile of chopped fish and hash browns.

After dinner, I notice that Sturgis has unpacked his paper bags. He's lined up his paperbacks on the shelf I cleared for him, and in front of the books is a neat row of cassettes. The books mostly have dragons or spaceships on the covers. I think a few of them have dragons *and* spaceships. For that matter, so do a lot of the cassettes.

My baseball cards are in shoe boxes on top of the bookcase. I used to be obsessed with them, sorting them and resorting them and memorizing their details and making teams out of batches and pitting them against each other using dice and rules I don't remember. It's weird how you wake up one day and don't care as much anymore, but that's kind of what happened. I still take good care of them, though, and look at them once in a while.

"I thought you might want to see my baseball cards," I say to Sturgis, setting the boxes out on the bed.

He looks at me for a moment, twisting his lip the way he does sometimes.

"Sure, I can look at them if you want," he finally says.

Sometimes I sort the cards by teams, sometimes alphabetically, and sometimes by year. These days I have them sorted by position. I like catchers the best, so I start with those. Mike Piazza. Ivan Rodriguez. Jorge Posada. A. J. Pierzynski. Bengie Molina. A Joe Mauer rookie card. I even have a Yogi Berra card from the 1960s that my dad gave me for Christmas. He gave me Yogi's book and planted that card in the middle as a surprise. Sturgis nods at each of them, but I might have been showing him a stamp collection for all he cares.

"Do you want to see my card?" he asks.

"You have cards, too?"

"Just one," he says. "Let me get it." He rummages in his bag and comes up with a battered book about motorcycle maintenance. He opens it and removes a card wrapped in tissue paper. He hands me the card.

It's ten years old, for a pitcher named Carey Nye of the Baltimore Orioles. He's a gloomy-looking guy, tall and lanky like Randy Johnson, with long hair and a mustache. I'm not sure I ever heard of him. His stats aren't that impressive. Then I remember Sturgis's comment from last night.

"Is this your dad?"

"It's a real collector's item, right?" He laughs and takes the card back, folding it into the square of paper and putting it in the book.

"Well, thanks for showing me," I tell him, trying not to sound either sarcastic or patronizing, and failing on both counts.

I suddenly feel like I've caught both ends of a double-header, with a marathon in the middle. It's only 8:00, but I brush my teeth, get undressed, and drop into bed. Sturgis is still up, reading by the overhead lamp, as I fade off to sleep. When I wake up in the middle of the night to use the bathroom, the light's still on. Sturgis is sound asleep, cuddling a homeowner's guide to landscape construction.

"You know," I tell Sturgis as we scrape around in the mud that Friday. We're done digging the ditch, which now runs across two of the property lines in an *L*. Frank wasn't happy with the job we'd done; the line of the ditch was ragged, its width and depth irregular. So now we're scraping it, evening out the sides, getting it ready for the concrete lining. "It's not just that it's killing my back and shoulders. It's not just the muddy wetness of it either. It's the mind-numbing boringness of it all."

Sturgis is working at his usual clip, a few paces away.

"I don't know how anyone does it," I say. "I mean, it's one thing to dig mud nine or ten hours a day for a whole week, but how about doing that day in, day out for months or even years? In the *rain*, no less? It's really something."

He's not listening to me, but I've found that complaining helps pass the time, so I do it anyway.

The guys order pizza for lunch. Sturgis and I have been

eating our lunch on the roof every day, enjoying the view. We figure it'll be pretty messy carrying pizza up the ladder, so we eat in the tent.

There's this guy, Peter, who joins us at our table. I've noticed him before. He's the shortest guy I've ever seen doing construction, like maybe five foot two. He's also got something messed up with one of his hands. There's no proper fingers on it, just little stubs. I've seen him holding nails while he pounds them in, using power tools, whatever. He handles the pizza just as easily as we do, too.

"You're the boss's son, right?"

"Yeah." I guess word gets around.

"My son could work, too. Peter Junior. He's your age but strong as an ox. Do you think you could talk to your father?"

"I don't know," I tell him honestly. "I think there are laws and stuff. You can have family work for you, but you can't hire other kids until they're older." Besides, I don't need another kid showing me up all the time, is what I'm thinking.

Peter looks confused. "You mean both of you are family?"

"In a manner of speaking," says Sturgis.

For a while, we just eat pizza without talking. One nice thing about this job has been the free food, although I guess it really isn't free to me since my dad pays for it.

"So do you boys have plans for the weekend?" Peter finally asks.

"Don't know," says Sturgis. "Maybe read or watch TV."

"I think it might rain," I add. It's the oldest and lamest joke in Moundville.

"Right. The rain," Peter says seriously. "I live in Sutton myself, so I don't get it all the time, but I'm originally from Sinister Bend, so . . ."

"That's too bad."

"Yeah," he says. "Our family lost everything in the flood. Well, we didn't have that much, but I was a kid. It was scary."

"Do they know why it keeps raining?" Sturgis asks. "I mean, there must be a scientific explanation."

I start in with my whole theory about Walt Dropo of Detroit and percentages and luck. I don't think either Sturgis or Peter buys it.

"Well, my grandma says an old Indian guy cursed it," says Sturgis.

"She must mean Ptan Tanka," says Peter. "He said dire things were in store for this town."

"It had something to do with the Sioux Uprising, right?" I offer. "I mean the Dakota War?"

"Not the war itself but what came after. The natives were sent away, to live on a reservation in South Dakota. People who had lived here for centuries."

"I'm sorry," I say. I am, too. I wasn't here, and I don't think my ancestors were either, but I'm sorry anyway.

"Come on," Lou suddenly calls over from the other end of the table. Lou has been around a long time and is one of Frank's best buddies. "Don't start in with that Indian curse nonsense."

"It's not nonsense!" Peter sort of bangs on the table. "I'm just talking about history."

"Anyway, the rain is caused by that hydroelectric dam upriver," someone else says. "The power company pays the government off so they won't look into it."

"That's what I think!" Ted or Tom or whatever his name is shouts. "The dam screwed up the local ecosystem."

"Hey, hey!" Frank raises his voice just one notch above normal indoor voice, and everyone listens. "No talking about the weather. That's the rule, okay?" Moundville is the one place on earth where it's not a safe topic for conversation.

Most of the guys nod, and it looks like things will calm down, but then Lou mutters something and Peter throws a wadded-up napkin at him, cursing. Pretty soon they're shoving each other and everyone is joining in, sticking up for Lou.

"I said knock it off!" Frank steps between them. They stop but keep glaring at each other. "Peter, I've talked to you before. You've had warnings. What is it going to take? Do I have to let you go?"

Peter crumples. "I'm sorry. I got carried away. Please don't fire me."

"Come on, Frank," one of the guys says softly. "You know he's got a family."

Frank throws his hands up in surrender.

"All right, all right." He wags his finger in Peter's face. "One more fight, though, and you're gone. I mean it' this time."

"Thanks," Peter says with a sniff.

Frank turns to Lou and the others. "Peter is going to stay on this crew. I don't want anyone messing with him just to get him in trouble."

"But he threw something at me," Lou complains.

"It was a balled-up napkin, you sissy," one of the guys reminds him. Everyone laughs.

"Still. I thought we had one of those zero-tolerance policies."

"You called me a dirty name," says Peter. "There should be zero tolerance for that, too."

"No more throwing anything, names or napkins." Frank's voice is now two notches above normal. You don't hear a peep out of anyone.

"All right, Frank," a few guys mutter.

"I wasn't asking for consensus. Lunch is over. Everyone, get back to work." The guys start filing out. Frank grabs Peter's arm as he walks by.

"You're on probation. Get a shovel and help the kids." The men howl with laughter. Apparently, working with me and Sturgis is a good punishment.

Peter grabs a shovel and digs like he's got to hit China by dusk.

"I think Lou deserves to be digging as much as you," says Sturgis.

"He's in pretty good with Frank," I tell them. "You don't want to mix it up with Frank's buddies. I've been around long enough to know that."

44

"You're right. I should know better than to argue with that fathead." Peter starts to smooth the sides of the ditch with his shovel.

"So are you an Indian?" Sturgis wonders.

"I'm part Sioux. A lot of people from Sinister Bend are . . . or were. That name is inaccurate, though, just like 'Indian.' Our family didn't pay much attention to our heritage, but lately I've become interested in my roots. I've been reading about Native American spirituality."

"I'm part Indian, too," says Sturgis. "A small part," he adds. He points at his face, maybe showing us the features that best reflect that aspect of his heritage.

"How did you get that scar?" Peter asks bluntly. "Were you attacked by an animal?" I'd been wanting to know for a few days, and Peter asks just like that. I'm impressed.

Sturgis's eyes widen. "Yeah. It was a wolf dog, actually. Part wolf, part dog."

"All dogs come from wolves. How did it happen?"

"When I was little, we had this big wolf dog named Sammy. I used to play catch with him, throwing tennis balls as far as I could into the woods. He'd always find them and bring them back, even if they went into a hole or some water or something. He was a great dog."

I'm kind of jealous. I've always wanted a dog, but dogs aren't exactly practical around here, so we just have Yogi.

"My dad trained Sammy to fight other dogs, though," says Sturgis. "Sammy was a great fighter. He won lots of fights."

"Dogfights are awful," I say without thinking.

"Oh, I agree." Sturgis nods. "It was my dad's idea, not mine. Anyway, my dad brought me to one of Sammy's fights. It was in the dirt basement of this bar in Sutton. We were right in front, surrounded by maybe a hundred guys, all making bets on which dog would win. I'd never seen Sammy fight and couldn't imagine him fighting. Once he was in the ring, though, he knew what to do. The other dog was bigger, but Sammy was faster and got his licks in."

"It's not the size of the dog in the fight; it's the size of the fight in the dog," says Peter. It's a kind of bumper sticker thing to say, but he has a point.

"Well, that big dog did get a piece of him," Sturgis continues. "I was scared and yelled Sammy's name. Sammy turned when I called him, and the other dog tore right into him, going for his throat. I jumped into the ring to save Sammy, but the other dog jumped on me, too. Maybe would have killed me, but my dad grabbed that dog and threw him off of me.

"There I was, bleeding all over the place, and these guys were just yelling at me for stopping the fight and yelling at my dad for letting me get in the way. Anyway, it was already over for Sammy. He was on his side, bleeding, and not breathing."

He says all this matter-of-factly, like it's something he's seen in a movie.

"The wolf attacked you to test you." Peter holds two of his stumpy fingers to Sturgis's face. "He wanted to make sure you could handle his power. He left his mark on you."

"Really?" Sturgis touches his own scars thoughtfully.

I don't put much stock in Peter's theory. That dog didn't try to test Sturgis; it tried to kill him. I don't say anything, though. I don't want to argue with Peter and get him in more trouble. Besides, if it makes Sturgis feel better about his face, what's the harm?

"I have a mark, too," says Peter. He pulls up his shirt-sleeve and shows us a horrible scar on his arm. It looks like a bear tried to take his arm off or something.

"Wow! How did that happen?"

"Cougar," he says with obvious pride.

"You got attacked by a cougar?"

"I was foolish once." He might as well be talking about a speeding ticket. I wonder if I'm the only one who's made it through life without getting mauled by an animal. I guess I'll have to find a bear and let it take a swipe at me if I want to fit in.

Frank and all his crew are coming with shovels. Peter begins digging furiously, to show he's a hard worker.

"Afternoon break is over," says Frank in a friendly way, clapping me on the shoulder with his big hand. "Come on, champ, let's dig. We're not going home until we finish this house."

I hope we can make short work of it and go home early.

Sturgis has finally slowed down, though. He throws up a few thoughtful shovelfuls of mud now and then, and that's all.

Chapter 5

"There was a fight at work today," Sturgis tells my dad on the drive home.

My dad looks anxious. "Nobody swung a shovel at anyone, did they?"

"No, no." I wish I could kick Sturgis from the front seat. "Just an argument. It was no big deal." I don't tell him that it nearly turned into a fistfight. I don't want to get anyone in trouble. "Frank took care of it."

"Whew," he says. "Good thing nobody swung a shovel at anyone. I don't need that kind of trouble. So what was it about?"

"The rain," says Sturgis.

"Of course," says my dad. "I bet one side said we're cursed."

"Yeah."

"And somebody else blames the dam?"

"Yeah."

"I've never heard such foolishness," says my dad. "Curse this, dam that. I say curse them all and dam them all." He chuckles at his own joke.

"Why does it rain, then?" asks Sturgis.

"Who knows? I'll let the other guys run around with their prayer books and candles, their balloons and charts. I just say, 'When it rains, sell umbrellas.'" It's my dad's favorite saying, kind of like "When life throws you lemons, make lemonade" and "Seize the day" wrapped into one slogan. It's not such a bad motto, if you sell umbrellas.

Steve calls me Saturday, wanting to play basketball. I'm sore all over from digging, but I decide to go anyway. For one thing, I said I would. For another, I miss hanging out with those guys.

"Want to shoot some hoops?" I ask Sturgis.

"I don't really know how."

"We'll show you. We just mess around anyway."

"I guess I'll come if you want me to."

I lend him some of my gym clothes. Also, my old basketball shoes, which are at least a size too small.

"My feet hurt," he says.

"Sorry."

We put our raincoats on over our shorts. I usually just shower and dress when I get home. I'm not a big fan of the rec center locker rooms—they typically look like they've been used by a bunch of bears in a big hurry.

Nothing is very far from anything else in Moundville, so we walk to the rec center, which they put next to the school so the kids could use it for gym class. I point out the school to Sturgis.

"The school only goes through sixth grade," I tell him. "What grade are you in anyway?"

"Not sure. I haven't been in a while."

"What?"

He shrugs. "Just haven't."

Steve and the other guys are already shooting baskets inside. The other guys are Miggy, Tim, and Ty. We hang out together pretty often. People at school might call us the jocks, but we're barely enough to make a basketball team, so it's not much of a clique.

"Hey, what happened to your face?" Tim asks when he sees Sturgis.

"Dude!" Steve shakes his head at Tim. "You don't just ask a guy something like that."

"What?" Tim gestures at his own face. "I'm just asking."

"I know you're just asking, and that's what I'm telling you a guy doesn't just do."

"It was a wolf," Sturgis says. Steve and Tim forget their argument and look at him in disbelief.

"Yeah, right!" says Ty.

"It's true," I tell them, even though I only half believe it myself.

"Man, how did you get bit by a wolf?" asks Miggy.

"He was bringing a basket to his grandma," I tell him. "What do you think?" They all crack up and don't bother asking any more questions. It helps the joke that Sturgis is still wearing his bright red raincoat with the hood.

We only have a part of the gym reserved. They cut it up into eighths on weekends, but there's a hoop in every section and enough room to play three-on-three.

Sturgis is a pretty good shot, sinking baskets from all over the court. He doesn't know the rules, though, and the other guys keep calling him out for blocks and hand checks.

"Man, does this game have a lot of rules," he complains, bouncing the ball, hard. The ball rebounds and smacks Ty in the face.

"No way!" says Tim.

"That's a T!" says Miggy.

"Sturgis, you can't do stuff like that," I tell him. "Miggy's right. It's a technical foul."

"It's a stupid game anyway," says Sturgis. His face is red, making his scar stand out more. "I quit." He grabs his raincoat from the corner where he left it and heads for the door.

"Dude, come on," I say, trying to keep up with him.

"My feet hurt anyway," he says. "You have small feet." He bangs out the front door and is gone.

After the game, Steve and I go get a pop in the vending area.

"So what's his deal anyway?" Steve wants to know, meaning Sturgis. I start to explain that he's a foster kid and who knows what he's been through, but I'm distracted by a couple of girls. One is kind of tall with brown hair—I think her name is Shannon—and she's with a shorter girl I've never seen before.

"Do you know her?" I ask Steve, subtly pointing out the shorter girl.

"What, do you assume I know every black girl in Mound County?"

"Yep."

"Well, her name is Rita," he says with a sigh. "She lives here but goes to school in Sutton. That's why you don't know her. I know her because my mom sold them their house." Steve's mom is a real estate agent. She's one of the flippers my dad talks about. She buys up derelict houses in Moundville, fixes them up, and sells them to people from Sutton looking for cheaper places to live. I bet she makes a load of money, but Steve says she started doing it because she felt sorry for those houses.

"You've met her, then?"

"We had dinner with them one time."

"You like her?"

"She's all right," he says. "Kind of a book snob." I want to ask him what this means, but the girls walk right by us, so I change the subject.

Sturgis wakes me up Sunday morning by flipping on the lights.

"Hey, a little warning next time!" I blink, trying to get used to the light.

He's being quite a jerk these days, I think. First he fights with my friends, then he sulks all night and barely talks to me. Now he's waking me up at the crack of dawn. Well, more like the crack of 9:00 a.m. Still, it's a weekend.

"Sorry," he says. "I need to see myself."

He's wearing a new pair of slacks and polo shirt. My dad took him shopping yesterday. You can still see the crease mark across the middle of his shirt, so he tries to press it out with his thumb.

"Where you going?" I ask. "You got a date or something?"

"I'm going to go see my grandma."

I half laugh, remembering the Red Riding Hood business from yesterday. "Seriously, what's up?"

"I am serious. My grandma is in a home, and I'm going to go see her."

"Oh."

"Don't you ever go see your grandma?"

As he combs his hair, I tell him how my dad's father passed away and his mom lives in Arizona, and how I never see my mom's parents anymore because I never see my mom anymore.

He finishes dressing and starts to put on his new sneakers with his slacks.

"I've got some nice dress shoes if you want," I tell him.

"Another day with pinched feet? No thanks."

"They're a little big for me, though." I climb out of bed and find him the shoes.

"These aren't too bad," he says, putting one on, then the other. "Yeah, I can deal with these."

"You look pretty sharp," I tell him.

"Just have to go get the basket of goodies ready," he jokes.

By the time I've had my own shower and pop into the kitchen, he's gone, and so is my dad. There's a note on the marker board on the fridge—"Back this afternoon"—and that's it. There's also a marker drawing of a little smiley face wearing a baseball cap. My dad has drawn those since I was a kid. I think it's supposed to be me.

I have toaster waffles and frozen sausage cooked in the microwave, then play on the computer until 1:30, when there's finally a baseball game on—an interleague game with the Cubs and White Sox. My official favorite team is the Tigers this year, but I always end up watching the Cubs because their games are all on cable.

The Cubs score seven runs in the bottom of the first inning, and for the rest of the game, any time the Sox mount a little comeback, the Cubs come right back and score a few runs themselves.

Dad and Sturgis get home around the seventh inning. They've been grocery shopping. Sturgis hauls a couple of bags into the kitchen.

"How was your grandmother?" I ask him.

"What big teeth she has," Sturgis jokes before heading back to the bedroom to change.

"Who's playing?" my dad asks.

"Chicago and Chicago," I tell him, even though he can see for himself.

"The old 'city serious,' as Ring Lardner used to call it." He sees the score is thirteen to ten. "Pitchers' duel, huh?"

"Yep. National League baseball at its finest."

"Well, I guess I better think about dinner," he says, heading off for the kitchen. "They had liverwurst on sale. I have something special planned!"

"Then I better *not* think about dinner," I mutter.

We start on a new job on Monday. Peter is still working with us on ditch duty.

"Did you talk to your father about giving my son a job?" he asks me.

"No, I didn't think about it. Anyway, laws and stuff, you know."

"I just wondered," he mutters, but I feel like he's looking at me a little sideways, mad that I didn't do it, laws or no laws.

Sturgis and Peter work about twenty feet away from me, the two of them doing ten times as much work as me by myself. They're whispering like long-lost cousins, probably about curses and sacred land and totem animals and who knows what else. I don't know if it's because I'm obviously zero percent Native American or because I'm the boss's kid or because I've never been snacked on by a wild animal, but they don't bother to include me.

I'm a bit skeptical about all of it. I'm also feeling left out.

"Hey, something's been bugging me," I holler over at them.

"Who, me?" asks Sturgis.

"No, Peter," I say. I haul my shovel over to where they're digging.

"So this Tutankhamen guy," I say.

Peter furrows his brow. "You mean Ptan Tanka?"

"Whatever his name is. Why did his curse take so long to kick in? If it's true, I mean, about his curse and the rain?"

"First of all, I never said it was a curse," Peter says simply.

"People twist the story around and leave out the most important part."

"What's that?"

"The fact that Ptan Tanka had a son. His name was Ptan Teca. Ptan Teca was a great athlete. He could run faster and jump higher than any other boy. He could swim further underwater, throw stones harder, and climb trees more nimbly. The boy was amazing.

"Ptan Teca was also a natural at the settlers' game of baseball. He could hit a ball a mile, then run out and catch it before it hit the ground. He pitched so fast the batter couldn't even see the ball. That became his best and favorite sport.

"When Ptan Teca found out he had to move to the Dakota Territory, he was furious. He was nearly as famous for his temper as he was for his athletic feats. 'They can't make us leave,' he said. 'We were here first!' He was also bitter about giving up baseball—he wouldn't have anyone to play with on the reservation. 'They want me gone because I'm the best at their game,' he said. His anger turned to hatred, and he swore that he would make the white settlers pay for their mistake."

"It wasn't really their fault, though," I protest. "The settlers in Moundville didn't make the laws."

"Ptan Teca decided everyone was his enemy," Peter explains. "He was mad at the white settlers for not opposing the law, and he was mad at his own tribe for not putting up a fight. He was also mad at the Dakota who did fight, because the new laws were a response to their rebellion. He was so mad he couldn't see straight."

"So it was the kid who cursed the place?" I ask.

"I never said there was a curse," Peter reminds us. "What happened was, Ptan Tanka woke up at dawn to discover his son was missing. Ptan Teca liked to go running or swimming early in the morning, but it was extremely cold that day and Ptan Tanka was worried.

"Ptan Tanka went out to look for his son and saw the boy's clothes lying in a pile by the bend in the river. He must have gone swimming, but there was no sign of him. Ptan Tanka stripped and entered the freezing cold water. He swam miles in either direction, searching underwater for any sign of his son. He would have searched until he drowned or froze to death if his wife and friends had not found him and dragged him to the fire to warm him. A group of natives and settlers formed a search party, but they never did find the body."

"That's pretty sad," says Sturgis.

"But what does it have to do with us?" I want to know. I don't know anybody stupid enough to swim in the Narrows River, even when it's warm. The river is flat-out dangerous.

Sturgis glowers at me.

"What?" I ask. "I was just wondering what it had to do with us, is all. Not that it wasn't an awful thing to happen to anyone. Did Ptan Tanka curse us because he was mad over losing his son?"

"Let me finish the story," Peter replies. "The search party came back and told Ptan Tanka his son was lost. Ptan Tanka hung his head in sorrow and spoke in a low growl. He said that dark times were ahead. He said that there would be vengeance, but he didn't say what kind. That's where the story of the curse was born."

"Sounds like a curse to me," I say.

"I think it was more of a warning," Peter explains. "Ptan Tanka didn't believe his son was dead, see. He thought his son had entered the spirit world and would harness its power to wreak his revenge. That's what the prophecy was about."

"But that still doesn't explain why it took so long to kick in," I realize. "It just started raining over twenty years ago."

"You're making one really big assumption," he says.

"What's that?"

"That the rain is Ptan Teca's revenge."

"Well, if it wasn't, then why are we talking about him?"

Peter looks thoughtfully up at the sky instead of digging. "Not much rain right now," he says. "Good time for a break." He heads off to the tent for some coffee, ignoring my question.

"Maybe that story does have something to do with us," Sturgis whispers after Peter is gone.

"You don't mean you believe all that business about a kid entering the spirit world."

"Well, Peter believes it," he says, and trots off to the portable toilet.

"So what?" I say to nobody. Lots of people believe lots of things. Curse this and dam that, as my dad says. What nobody gets is that it's all percentages.

I look up at the sky and think I see some of the clouds blowing away and maybe a little sunshine peeking through.

That happens sometimes. You learn pretty young not to start planting sunflowers just because the rain lets up a little. I stick the shovel firmly in the mud, take off my raincoat and hang it on the shovel handle, and go to the tent for some water.

When I step back outside, the rain has stopped completely.

The clouds are clearing, revealing a stunning blue sky. The guys on the roof drop what they're doing and reel back in astonishment. Up and down the street, people leave their houses and offices to look up in wonder.

I've imagined this moment many times, and I always thought people would shout and skip and sing and dance in the streets, like so many extras in a musical. I thought I would run to the ballpark, with its rotting benches and ruined field. I would have my shin guards and chest protector on, my bat and glove ready, and I would stretch out in the muddy outfield and wait for the grass to grow back.

Instead, my stomach is in a knot and I can't move. Lou is crying, gesturing at the now-cloudless sky and trying to speak to Frank, but Frank turns away, overcome. I realize we're all scared.

Sturgis glances up, takes his shovel, and starts scooping mud from his wheelbarrow back into the ditch.

"We might as well fill this back in," he says.

Chapter 6

Frank says we should take the day off. Either the rain will pick up again and fall for another twenty-odd years, or it's really over. If it starts raining again, we'll waste the only sunny afternoon in years; if it doesn't, our jobs are obsolete anyway. So for maybe the first time in history, something is called off on account of no rain.

"So how do your percentages explain this?" Sturgis asks when we get home.

"What do you mean? Statistics *completely* explain it."

"You said the statistics were why it was raining. Now they're why it's *not* raining. That makes a lot of sense!"

"It does." I go through the whole explanation again, using Walt Dropo as an example.

"So Walt Dropo is Moundville, and base hits are rain?"

"Exactly."

"All right. So what does that have to do with it not raining anymore?"

"Because after Walt Dropo got twelve hits in a row, he wasn't guaranteed a hit the next time. That's why."

"I still don't get it."

"It's called a gambler's fallacy. It's like if you're playing roulette and there's a bunch of reds in a row. A gambler might think it's going to be red next time, or maybe that there's going to be a run of blacks. Either way, he's wrong. The odds are exactly the same for every spin."

"I read this James Bond novel where this casino had a magnet under the wheel and could freeze the ball wherever they wanted it. I'd put my money on red."

"If it's fixed, you're going to lose either way," I remind him.

"Oh, right." He looks thoughtful. "Anyway, I don't see what that has to do with this."

"Every day is a new day. The past doesn't matter. That's all I'm saying."

"If that's what the statistics think, the statistics are dumb." He grabs his fantasy book and stalks off to read it. With all the junk he reads about elves and wizards, it's no wonder he can't think scientifically.

My dad is not much in the mood for cooking, so he sprinkles some frozen peas on a frozen pizza and throws it in the oven.

"Peas on pizza?" I ask when I see it.

"You need your vegetables," he says sharply.

The pizza is burned on the edges and cold in the middle. We eat it anyway, seeing how upset he is.

"Up to my nose in debts," my dad mutters, and "Good luck getting anyone to honor their contracts," and "My life's work is down the tubes."

"When it rains, sell umbrellas," I remind him.

"I did that!" he snaps. "It's not raining anymore, and I have a warehouse full of umbrellas."

"It might start raining again," Sturgis says helpfully.

"There's no reason it can't rain another twenty years, even. Percentagewise."

"He's right, Dad," I agree.

"Do you think?"

"Yeah. Absolutely."

"I hope you're right." My dad spends the rest of the evening taking calls from customers, all of them canceling their orders.

Later on, he yells at me that I have a phone call. I wonder if it's Steve. He probably wants to play baseball ASAP, before the rain starts again.

"Dude," I say into the phone.

"Well, hello there." It's my mother. She sounds a little tipsy. "I saw you on the late news."

"I was on the news?"

"Your town, silly. Good old Moundville." She laughs. "Mudville, USA. They said it stopped raining, just like that."

"Yep," I say, like it's no big deal.

"Who woulda thunk it?"

"Not me," I say. "Next thing you know, the Cubs will win the World Series."

She laughs. "Or maybe Moundville will even beat Sinister Bend! Hey, I sent you a postcard from Chicago. Did you get it?"

"Yeah. Thanks. I added it to the collection." She sent me a postcard from U.S. Cellular, though, not Wrigley Field.

"Anyway," she says, "I just wanted to say congratulations. Hey, tell your dad he can finally finish that baseball game. If they can round everyone up." She laughs again and starts singing "Take Me Out to the Ball Game."

Now I know she's tipsy.

"Well, thanks for calling." I hang up the phone right in the middle of the part about how she doesn't care if she never gets back.

The next day is the Fourth of July. It's a perfect day for it, too: sunny and not a drop of rain. Around noon, I get an itch to head outside and see what's going on.

"Want to go hang out downtown?" I ask Sturgis. He's on the couch, reading one of his paperback books.

"I don't think so," he says. "I've been wanting to reread this series for a while. Roger Zelazny." He looks at me hopefully, but I've never heard of the guy and don't care.

"You're going to hang out inside when it's actually not raining?"

He shrugs. "Inside's okay," he says. "I just kind of want to read."

"Didn't you say yourself that it would probably start up again? What if it's the only nice day for the next twenty-two years?"

"There's a short story like that by Ray Bradbury," he says. "It takes place on a planet where the sun comes out for a few hours every seven years. One kid spends the whole day locked in a closet."

"And you want to be that kid?"

"Yeah. I always identified with that kid."

My dad is in the office, messing with invoices or something.

"Want to go kick around town?" I ask him.

"Maybe later. I'm trying to figure out how to give everyone two weeks' severance pay without selling our house."

"Well, I'm going to head out," I tell him. "Just in case this is the one sunny day in my whole life. I don't want to be like the kid in the Roger Bradbury story." That sounds wrong, but whatever.

"All right. Have fun."

What a couple of sad sacks, I think as I bang out the door.

I'm glad to discover I'm not the only one eager to get out and enjoy the weather. People are setting up rusty old grills in their driveways, trying to light age-old charcoal. They're in the street, tossing Nerf footballs and Frisbees. One family has even dumped enough fresh sand in their muddy yard to have a go at volleyball.

It occurs to me that I don't really know everyone, the way you're supposed to in a small town. Everyone was inside all the time, and even outside they were hidden under hoods and umbrellas. I walk along, waving at all the neighbors and wishing I could halfway whistle. I'm just in that kind of mood.

Downtown, there's an impromptu block party. Most towns have them on the Fourth, but Moundville never has in my lifetime. Everyone packs off to Sutton or wherever for barbecue and fireworks. This year, everyone has gathered downtown.

There's a big grill going—who knows where they found it—and a snow cone machine and an ice cream truck and popcorn and cotton candy. There's a rock band playing in the ruins of the grandstand and a guy dressed like Uncle Sam, on stilts, making balloon animals for kids. It's strange to see all this among the washed-out buildings and gray mud. It reminds me of this weird painting I saw once, because the background is the same, like a desert on Pluto. Only instead of melting clocks and a dead walrus, there's kids eating cotton candy and an Uncle Sam making balloon animals.

"Hey, Roy!"

I turn around and see Steve.

"Nice day!" he says, grinning from ear to ear.

"I've seen nicer," I joke, but I'm grinning, too.

"I'm going to get bunnies for my baby sisters," he says. I wait while he puts in the request with Uncle Sam. "Two rabbits. One blue and one red."

"So where's your foster brother or whatever?" Steve wants to know while we're waiting.

"Sturgis? He's reading."

"Man. That's messed up."

"Well, he's only lived here like a week," I remind him. "This is no big deal for him."

Uncle Sam hands Steve the two balloon rabbits, and Steve hands one to me.

"For me?"

"Shut up. Come on."

We're walking through the crowd when we see the girls

from the gym. The one I noticed before turns around and smiles really adorably at both of us. I smile back, then remember I'm carrying a balloon bunny. I try to carry it casually, but it's just about impossible to carry a balloon bunny and be cool about it. The girls are whispering to each other, pointing and laughing.

"Remind me to beat you up later," I tell Steve.

"What for?"

"Just remind me."

We find Steve's family eating hot dogs and watching the band play.

"We saw a guy making balloon animals," Steve announces. We give the rabbits to Sheila and Shauna. I glance around, hoping those two girls can see us, but they're gone.

The twins are excited, of course, and want to tell me all about how the sun came out and the rain went away, and how all the kids at day camp went out and played tag, and how the teacher didn't care that they were all covered with mud from head to toe by the end of the day.

Steve's dad hands me a hot dog loaded with mustard and onions, but no ketchup.

"Thanks. Just the way I like it."

"I know. I don't forget a man who knows how to eat a hot dog."

There are more hot dogs after that, and pop and caramel corn and ice cream. It's kind of a blur. Steve and I join some guys kicking a soccer ball around in the street, then supervise a three-legged race by kids eight and under, which is won by his sisters.

The main thing everyone talks about is rain—why it stopped and whether it will start up again. Since he's pretty much the smartest guy I know, I ask Mr. Robinson.

"I'm a history teacher, not a weatherman," he says with a shrug. "All I know is, it's a darned good day for a picnic."

Just when it starts to get dark, the mayor gets up in the old grandstand.

"I better get a few words in here before it starts to rain," says the mayor, looking up at the perfectly cloudless sky. The crowd titters a bit. The mayor holds out his hand, palm up. "I think I felt a drop!" The crowd hoots and hollers.

"Well, it's been a long wait," he says. "It's been a long wait, and I'm amazed and proud at how many people stayed here in town, waiting it out together. They must know what I always knew, which is that this is a special town. A town worth waiting out a little rain."

Scattered applause. Whistles. Hoorahs.

I search the crowd for those two girls, but I don't see them.

"The pessimists out there say it's going to start again any second, but I think we're in for better times. Moundville will be . . . Well, I almost said this town would be great again, but it never stopped being great!"

Now the applause is more thunderous. People like being told they're great.

"Either way, the forecast now is sunshine. So enjoy your Fourth of July, and enjoy the fireworks. And we'll meet back here next year for more fun in the sun. Maybe we'll even have baseball!" There's an especially loud swell of applause, with cheering and foot stomping and hollering. The mayor waves goodbye and walks off the grandstand.

"Yeah!" I trade a high five with Steve. If there is baseball, we're pretty sure we'll be in it.

"I can't wait for that," says Steve's dad. "Just like the good old days. If we can find someone to beat us, that is." He lets out a loud guffaw, and some of the guys standing around us join in.

The fireworks are nothing by Sutton standards, but I'm blown away. Really, I am. A brilliant flash of colored lights against a tapestry of stars. I'm awed by them. I'm usually not a big fireworks guy, but I'm in the mood this year. I think it's because it's not raining, and because a cute girl might have smiled at me.

I walk home alone and find the house empty. I guess that my dad and Sturgis went out to see the fireworks and will be home any second. I kick back on the couch and watch a sports news show while Yogi nestles against me.

Dad and Sturgis get home about an hour later.

"Where were you guys?" It sounds like I'm the dad, waiting up for the kids.

"We went to watch the fireworks in Sutton," my dad says.

"There were fireworks here, too."

"Oh. Well, these were great!" says my dad. "You should've seen them!"

"Yeah," says Sturgis, flopping down next to me and reaching for his book. Yogi abandons me to nuzzle Sturgis's arm.

"The fireworks here were good, too," I tell my dad. I think it's weird that they'd head off to Sutton instead of seeing what was going on here in Moundville. I just don't get it.

"Well, we didn't know they'd have fireworks here," says my dad. "It's not that far to Sutton. Oh, and, Roy, that reminds me. We need to talk."

"About St. James Academy?" I guess.

"Right."

"I don't have to go," I tell him. "It's no big deal."

"It is a big deal," he says. "But I don't see how we can swing it. I'm really sorry."

"It's all right. I understand."

"I'll call them tomorrow." He gives me a one-armed hug before going off to his bedroom.

"Mind if I mute this?" Sturgis asks. "I'm kind of reading."

"Whatever."

He turns off the sound, and I look blankly at the screen while a bearded guy yells at the camera about something.

I'd really planned on going to St. James Academy, even if it was never officially official, so it's hard to adjust. I can't imagine getting very good coaching from a guy who's mostly a math teacher or something and just coaches on the side.

Sutton spends loads of money on football and basketball, but nothing on baseball.

The whole mess pushes the fireworks and Rita right out of my head.

I can't sleep that night. I'm wound up, thinking about everything.

"Hey, Sturgis," I whisper. He's a pretty sound sleeper and doesn't respond.

I get out of bed and creep down the hall to my father's office. I turn on the desk light and fire up the computer. Yogi finds me there and jumps into my lap to help.

I check my e-mail, but there's nothing good. Check the baseball standings and see how Detroit's doing. They're on a tear this summer, which is way out of character for them.

Then I get an idea. I've been wondering about something. I Google "Carey Nye" and get a few hundred results: player pages from baseball sites, autographed balls and jerseys on eBay, and so on. I follow the first link to a page on the official Orioles site. It's got a picture and some stats and a short biography.

"Carey Nye was once considered a top prospect in the Orioles organization," the page reports. "He led the AAA Rochester Red Wings in wins and strikeouts one season and once pitched a no-hit shutout. He was not as successful in the majors. In his first year as a starter, he posted three wins and nine losses. He was transferred to the bullpen, where he was effective for short stints but inconsistent."

Most of the other links all have the same information: a line of stats, maybe a brief description of a young pitcher who failed to live up to his promise. Nothing about his family.

So I Google "Carey Nye" and "Sturgis" at the same time and get exactly one result. It's some guy's biker blog, where he's posted a bunch of photos from the big motorcycle rally they have every year in Sturgis, South Dakota. There's a lot of pictures, so the page kind of goes on forever. Fat guys with big beards and tattoos sitting on Harleys. That kind of thing.

I figure the page came up because Sturgis is the name of the town. There must be other guys named Carey Nye in the world. I'm about to quit scrolling when I see his picture, though. He looks just like his baseball card, except he's wearing a denim jacket with the sleeves cut off and no shirt. With him is a kid, about four years old. His face is in the shadows, but I can tell it's Sturgis because of his long arms and legs.

"Carey Nye of the Baltimore Orioles," the caption says. (He wouldn't have been an Oriole by that time, though.) "Named his kid Sturgis. HOW COOL IS THAT?"

I click back to Google and do another search on Carey Nye, wondering what happened to him. None of those biographies have what happened after he got cut by the Orioles. He just vanished off the face of the earth.

I find the answer in an old column on the *Sporting News* site. The article is basically about how pro athletes don't always get away with murder. The author mostly talks about some football player who went to prison, but he mentions a few others in passing.

"It barely made headlines even in Baltimore when former Oriole Carey Nye was convicted for murdering a man in a bar fight," the article says, "but he was a player the fans in Baltimore would rather forget about anyway, even without a little recreational manslaughter on his résumé."

I feel almost guilty, nosing into Sturgis's life like that. It just didn't occur to me that his dad was in prison. I clear the browser history to cover my tracks and return to bed, my head spinning.

I wonder if my dad knows all that. I think he must. The foster care people would have told him. How long would his dad be in prison? Did Sturgis ever see him? How did his mom die?

I lie there, wondering, while Sturgis sleeps. He snores lightly, with an occasional whimper, like the puppy I never had.

Chapter 7

In the morning, I'm falling asleep in my bowl of cereal. Sturgis has already finished a couple of bowls and is back on the couch, reading his book.

"Want to go play catch?" I ask him after breakfast. It looks like another gorgeous rainless day is in the making.

"Why not?" he says, setting the book down. So it's easier to get him off the couch than I thought.

We could throw the ball around in the patch of mud we call a yard, but we decide to walk down to the old ballpark instead, just to see how it's doing.

The ballpark is right downtown, so it's not a bad walk. There's a little business district across the streets on the first base side and right field. A hard-hit homer to dead center would land on the steps of the town hall. To the left is the old high school, which hasn't been used in my lifetime but still has offices and stuff.

"Darn hot," says Sturgis.

"Yes, it is," I say, "and humid."

The ballpark is a mess. You wouldn't even know it's a ballpark, except for the rotting bleachers and rusted-out backstop behind the plate, or at least where the plate *used* to be. The ground has mostly drained, thanks to the canals, but it's slimy, with puddles of water everywhere, and not a blade of grass. Swarms of gnats greet us with every step, and horseflies screech in our ears. The mud tries to suck off my shoes. It's disgusting.

"Will the grass grow back on its own?" I ask Sturgis.

"You're asking me?" He shrugs.

"Well, you're the major-league kid."

"My dad was a relief pitcher, not a groundskeeper."

I have my catcher's mitt and Sturgis has my fielder's glove—good thing we're both right-handed—and I've got an old, beat-up ball I don't care about. I hand it off to Sturgis and walk about forty paces.

"Show me what you got."

He zips it in and stings my hand.

"You have good stuff!" It must be in his blood, I think. His dad, the big leaguer.

"I do?"

"Sure. Throw it again, as hard as you can."

He rears back and lets it rip. The ball smacks into my glove like it's been shot from a cannon, even without a proper windup. Look out, Roger Clemens.

"You really never played baseball? You have a good arm."

"I used to throw tennis balls to my dog."

"Sammy?"

"Yeah."

"That was a long time ago," I remind him.

He shrugs. "I still throw sometimes."

"Throw what?"

"Rocks. Whatever."

He isn't so good at catching the ball. Even if I throw it right to him, he misses half the time.

"I usually don't have anyone to throw back at me," he explains.

We toss the old beanbag back and forth for a time, in the hazy sunshine, until the bugs and humidity get to us. Even with the bites and the burn, it feels great.

I half expect my dad to be making sacrifices to a rain god when we get home. Instead, he's signing the last batch of paychecks. He hands one to me and one to Sturgis.

I try to hand the check right back to him. "Keep it."

"But that's for you," he says.

I don't mean to get dramatic over what I know is only a drop in the bucket, but I don't want the check. It doesn't feel right, knowing about our new money problems.

Sturgis folds his own check and puts it into his pocket. He looks at us warily, hoping we didn't expect him to fork over the money.

"Just hold on to it for me." I give my dad the check. "I'll use it for baseball camp next year."

"All right." He puts the check in his front desk drawer. "It's right here when you want it," he says. I feel a little bit better. The money will sit in my dad's checking account, but Sturgis doesn't have to feel guilty for keeping his own hard-earned cash.

"Oh, were you out practicing already?" my dad asks, seeing the ball and gloves.

"Just playing catch. Sturgis here has a pretty good arm."

"Good, good," he says.

"Dad, do you think that grass will grow on its own in the ballpark, or will we have to plant it?"

"I imagine they'll have to seed it or sod it. Lots to do in that ballpark." He looks kind of thoughtful, then goes back to his work.

Dinner is chili dog pie, which is not as good as it sounds.

"So you like to play baseball, too?" my dad asks Sturgis.

"Sure," he says around a mouthful of canned chili, hot dog, and Tater Tots.

"Well, this used to be a big baseball town," my dad says. "When I was a kid, everybody wanted to play baseball."

"A lot of kids still want to play baseball," I tell my dad. "They just couldn't. They will now."

"You think so, huh?"

I tell him about what the mayor said, about playing baseball next year, and the big round of applause. People seem pretty psyched.

"Why would anyone have to wait until next year?" asks Sturgis.

"It's not just about baseball," my dad explains. "It's about tradition." He tells Sturgis the long history of baseball on the Fourth of July. Every year, Moundville and Sinister Bend would play, and every year, Moundville would lose.

"My dad was in the last baseball game ever played in Moundville," I tell Sturgis.

"Did you win?" Sturgis asks.

"Funny you should ask," my dad says. "We didn't win, but it's the first time in about a century we didn't lose."

"Hey, we should watch that game after dinner," I suggest. I sort of do it for my dad. I figure he needs a break from worrying about money, and he loves to watch that old video. He even had the whole thing dumped onto a DVD a while back.

"I don't know." My dad looks distracted. He's probably itching to get back to his spreadsheets.

"I was going to watch a show at seven," Sturgis says. I give him a friendly kick under the table. "Um, but let's watch the game instead," he says.

My dad grins. "I suppose."

Sturgis and I do the dishes while my dad finds the DVD. When we come out of the kitchen, the slightly blurry image of the ballpark the way it used to be flickers into view, deep green with sharp white lines, like I've never seen it. My dad collapses into his favorite chair, the remote control in his hand. Yogi clambers up to the arm of the chair and sits in a stately pose, looking like he ought to be in front of the New York Public Library.

"Bobby Fitz," my dad says with a happy sigh as the Moundville pitcher takes the mound. "Best baseball player I ever knew. He was going to be a superstar." To prove his point, Bobby Fitz makes short work of the Sinister Bend batters in the top of the first inning.

"So what happened to him?" Sturgis wonders. "Is he famous now?"

"Last I heard, he was selling insurance in Sutton."

"That's too bad."

"Hey, there's nothing wrong with that." My dad sounds a little defensive. "People in Sutton need insurance, too."

"I didn't mean anything," Sturgis says apologetically. "Anyway, let's watch this." He leans forward in his chair as the Bend pitcher takes the mound.

He's a tall, mean-looking boy with unkempt hair. He throws hard. Really hard. The ball seems to be smoking as he hurls it at the catcher.

"Bobby was our leadoff hitter, too," my dad points out as the first Moundville batter steps into the box. He knocks the first pitch over the pitcher's head for a base hit but is tagged out trying to stretch the single into a double. He limps off the field.

"Pulled his hamstring." My dad shakes his head, remembering. "What bad luck. Every year, something like that. Moundville was just flat-out cursed."

"I thought you didn't believe in curses," Sturgis reminds him.

"I don't believe in weather curses. Baseball curses are a whole nother ball of wax."

The Bend pitcher strikes out the next batter, and the

next kid comes to the plate. He's tall and blond, his hair long enough to stick out beneath his batting helmet. He looks at the pitcher with a big toothy grin, like he's not one bit scared. The pitcher zips in three pitches and strikes him out looking at a belt-high fastball.

"That was me," my dad tells Sturgis, who nods.

"I guessed," he says. "You look exactly like Roy."

The Sinister Bend team proceeds to knock the new Moundville pitcher around like a tetherball, while the Bend pitcher glides through the innings. It's eleven to zero by the middle of the fourth inning.

"Look at these clouds gathering." My dad freezes the frame so we can appreciate them. "It's starting to drizzle, see?" He indicates the vertical lines on the screen.

"I thought it was just the graininess of the old video," says Sturgis.

"Our coach had this great idea," says my dad. "He told us to play for the rain delay. The game wouldn't be official until the end of the fourth inning. If it was rained out, we could start over with a clean slate and a healthy pitcher. He told us to work the count, foul off pitches, and dawdle as much as possible."

We watch the first two batters ground out, and my dad comes up to bat.

I've counted his foul-offs every time I watch the video, but I always get a different number. We watch Dad foul off pitch after pitch. He hits balls into the stands, right down the line, everywhere but fair. The fans have to toss the balls back because they've run out. It slows the game down even more, while the rain picks up.

You can see the pitcher getting annoyed and tired, losing speed and control of his pitches. My dad even takes a few balls, mixed in with the fouls, until he has a full count. Then comes his famous base hit. He's just trying to protect the plate, but the ball stays fair. The crowd groans, then cheers as the ball gets past the third baseman.

We lose track of him as the camera follows the ball. The left fielder is running to field it but slips in the wet grass. The ball rolls to the fence. The center fielder bare-hands it but can't get a grip on it. The camera swoops back toward the infield. My dad has rounded the bases and comes home with no play at the plate. He's greeted by the rest of his team with high fives and slaps to the helmet. The pitcher throws his glove to the mound in disgust.

The umpires meet, and the screen flickers into blackness.

"What happened next?" asks Sturgis.

"That was that," my dad says. "The game was called for rain and never replayed."

"Well, now you can have the rematch," says Sturgis.

"Sinister Bend is long gone, though," I remind him.

"Anyway, we're all old now," says my dad. "Scattered far and wide, with bad backs and mortgage payments." Thinking about mortgage payments gets him fretting again, and he goes back to his office to mess with budgets on the computer.

⚐ ⚐ ⚐

"Hey, Sturgis, you ever have a girlfriend?" I ask him that night after the lights are out.

"With this mug?" he asks. I didn't think of that. I barely notice anymore.

"Hey, chicks dig scars."

"Yeah, right, they do."

"They do. I'm sure of it."

"What about you?" he asks. "Did you ever have a girl-friend?"

"Not really," I tell him. Last year, in sixth grade, I was go-ing with this girl for a few weeks. That's what they call it at my school, just going with someone. All it meant was that we had lunch together and she passed me notes. One day, one of those notes said she was breaking up with me, and that was that. I didn't lose any sleep over it.

"You got your eye on someone?" he asks.

"What makes you think that?"

"You wouldn't start talking about girls otherwise. You're trying to get the conversation around to how you like some-one."

"Yeah, I guess." I tell him about Rita, and how I've seen her but not talked to her, and how she smiled but it might have been at Steve. "Do you think a black girl would rather date a black guy?"

"Last time I looked at a calendar, it was 2000-something," he says. "That's not an issue anymore. This Rita girl probably digs you."

"How do you know?"

"'Cause look at you," he says. "You're a jock. You're decent-looking. You're a nice guy. You're the guy a girl would dig."

"Well, thanks. I guess if she says no, I have you as a backup plan."

"You dig scars, too?"

"Heck yeah. Rita has a bright red scar right across her head, and it makes her look like a baseball. That's why I like her."

He cracks up. I must be picking up my dad's gift of humor.

"She have any friends?" he wants to know. "The kind who dig scars?"

"I'll ask her the next time I talk to her," I tell him. "I mean, the first time I talk to her."

"All right," he says. He's out like a light again, and I'm left in the darkness for a while, wondering when that will be.

We work for the next few days, removing half-installed Rain Redirection Systems from houses. It's just Sturgis and me and my dad. My dad doesn't want to pay anyone to take down canceled orders and recover the materials, so we do it all by ourselves. That's how Sturgis and I finally get to work up on the roof. I like to imagine Rita will walk by one of those houses and see me glistening with sweat, doing a man's job, and maybe swoon right there on the sidewalk. No such luck, but thinking about it helps pass the time.

"Well, we're done with that," my dad says as we wrap

things up late on Friday evening. "I think my rain redirection business is officially done."

He doesn't feel like cooking again, which really isn't like him. We pick up a bucket of chicken on the way home. I don't mind one bit. I'm a big fan of takeout.

"What about that one?" I ask when we get home, pointing at the obsolete contraption of plastic sheeting on our own roof.

"Oh, right." My dad looks up at it in disgust. "We'll get it sooner or later."

We're barely through the door when my dad has the TV on and surfs through the channels until he finds a M*A*S*H marathon. Sturgis joins him on the couch this time, and they eat in the living room, not even using plates—just tossing their chicken bones back into the bucket and passing the little tubs of corn and potatoes back and forth.

"I love this one!" my dad says when one of the shows comes on. He points at the TV with a chicken leg and starts to explain to Sturgis how the actor playing a minor character went on to be someone else in a different TV show.

He hasn't been this happy since the rain stopped. I don't know if this is better or worse than stressing out about his business, but it's definitely messier.

Chapter **8**

It keeps on not raining. On Saturday, I call Steve and we head down to the park to chuck the ball around. I bring Sturgis, and Steve brings a bunch of guys, including Tim and Miggy. They nod hello to Sturgis, but I can guess they're a little peeved about the tantrum he threw at the rec center.

We don't have enough gloves to go around, so I hand mine off to Tim. It's good for a catcher to toughen up his hands anyway. Sturgis's pitches are a little hot to handle, though, even when he means to throw them soft. He doesn't say much, just catches the ball and throws it back, always with a little steam on it.

Tim and Miggy keep throwing the ball in the mud and over our heads. I show them how to put their fingers on the ball properly, and pretty soon they're throwing straight. Straighter anyway.

"When do we get to hit?" asks Kazuo. He's one of the new guys. I don't know him that well because he's a year behind me in school.

"I brought a bat," I tell him. "It'll be good to get some swings in."

First we have to pace out where the mound ought to be, then estimate where the bases are. We just draw Xs in the mud for the bases and kick a little mud around for the pitcher's mound.

I put on my catcher's mitt and get behind the so-called plate, and Steve throws some soft stuff at this other sixth grader named David. David swings and misses on the first five or six pitches. Finally, he makes contact, and the ball rolls through the mud, back to Steve.

"I got a hit!" he says, running to first base.

I laugh. "Only because we don't have a first baseman," I tell him. "Normally, you'd be out by a mile."

Kazuo has better instincts. He doesn't swing at every pitch, and when he does, he takes a good swing. He knocks what might be a bona fide hit up the middle, but he drops the bat and runs to third.

"You need to go *that* way," I yell to Kazuo, pointing at first base.

"Sorry," Kazuo says, looking bewildered. "I think I got confused because I was batting left-handed."

"You were batting *right*-handed," I tell him. "Don't you know left from right?"

"Well, sure," he says, but he sounds a little unsure.

"Wait a second," I say. "You said you were batting left. Do you mean you can also bat right? I mean, you were really batting right-handed, but do you mean you can also bat left?"

He looks more confused than ever.

"Can you bat both ways?" I ask him.

"Sure!" he says. "I can do everything both ways. I can write letters with both hands, draw, eat, everything. I can even throw both-handed. I think that's why I get confused. It's all the same to me."

Sturgis takes a few swings, too, but can't catch up with the pitch.

"Maybe he can scare the ball with his face," David says to Kazuo, who shakes his head and kicks at the ground in disgust. Sturgis turns and glares at them both. When he swings again, he's way out in front. He swears and drops the bat in the mud.

"Hey," I say, picking up the bat, wishing I had something to wipe off the mud.

"Sorry, Roy." He takes the bat from me and wipes the mud on his shorts before handing it back. "Can I pitch now?"

"Sure. Steve, let Sturgis pitch to you."

Steve trades places with Sturgis, and I signal for the fastball. Sturgis scorches one in there, and Steve steps back in surprise.

"Strike one!" I call.

"No way," Steve says, shaking his head.

"It had the corner." I toss the ball back to Sturgis and signal for another fastball over the plate. Sturgis throws one even harder, right in the zone. Steve flails at it and misses. I toss the ball back while Steve shakes his head in disbelief and tries to get better footing in the muddy batter's box.

"He throws hard," Steve says with respect.

I signal for a change-of-pace pitch, but Sturgis throws another fastball. Steve nails it but hits it foul.

"I got it!" David yells, running off to fetch it like an enthusiastic golden retriever.

I trek out to the mound to talk to Sturgis.

"You do know the signals, right?"

He looks at me as if I'm crazy.

"When I hold up one finger, I'm saying to throw a fastball," I explain. "When I hold up two fingers, it means throw a curveball. When I wiggle three fingers, it means throw a changeup. It's classic baseball stuff."

"A changeup?"

I sigh, not getting how he could throw so well and not know the basics of pitching. "Put another finger on the ball and throw it just like a fastball. The finger slows it down a smidgeon. It's called a change-of-pace pitch, or changeup for short."

"Oh, you mean a *junkball*." He wrinkles his nose like I've just asked him to throw a dog turd. "Why would I want to throw junkballs?"

"To fool that batter."

"Nah, I don't play that way. I don't need to trick anyone."

"It's part of the game," I explain. "It's not trickery, it's strategy."

David comes loping back with the ball and tosses it to Sturgis. Sturgis holds the ball with the right grip for a changeup and looks at me as if I am nuts. I notice for the first time how long his fingers are. The kid is born to pitch, I think. He has the hands of Mariano Rivera.

"Try it," I tell him.

I trot back to the plate and get in position. I wiggle my

fingers, and Sturgis tries the changeup. The ball lands about a foot in front of me.

"We'll work on that." I fetch the ball, wipe it off on my shirt, and toss it back.

Sturgis pitches another fastball. Steve gets under it and pops it straight up. I just park under it until it plops into my glove.

"My turn!" I flip the ball back to Sturgis and pass my catcher's gear to Steve. I'm eager to try hitting Sturgis's fastball.

I've been timing it mentally and give the first pitch a pretty good knock to deep short.

"Yeah!" I exclaim, pumping my fist on my way to first. "Move me over, Miggy!"

Miggy swings at the first pitch and bounces it right back to Sturgis. Sturgis realizes he has no first baseman to throw to and throws to me instead. Being a good sport, I catch it bare-handed and tag the bag to put Miggy out.

"I guess I can play first base now." Miggy takes the ball from me and tosses it back to Sturgis.

"Move me over, David!" I holler as he takes the bat and steps into the batter's box.

Sturgis throws one pitch, hard and inside, nailing David in the chest. He drops the bat with a whimper and rubs his chest. I'm not sure if it was a mistake or an on-purpose. I can't tell by looking at Sturgis. He just stands calmly on the mound, as if waiting for David to get back in the batter's box.

"I get to go to first," David finally says, and walks slowly to the base, still rubbing his sore chest, while I advance to second. I guess he moved me over, like I asked him to.

Kazuo steps back to the plate, and Sturgis quickly strikes him out. "Inning's over," he says. He strides off, giving David a quick look that says there was nothing accidental about that plunk. David looks away and kind of toes the ground, not wanting to get into a fight with a kid a head taller than him.

Steve is too excited to notice. "This is great! We should get teams together and play a game."

"We need to get this park cleaned up first," I point out. "We can't play a proper game in this mess."

"Ah, it's just a little grass and some dirt. No big deal."

When I get home, my father is in good spirits. He's chopping celery for what he calls his world-famous green bean chili. I know because of the green beans and cans of tomato soup on the counter. He's dropping bits of taco meat down to Yogi, who loves the stuff.

"Roy," he asks, "what does one do when it rains?"

"Sell umbrellas!" I say automatically.

"What if it *doesn't* rain?" he asks.

"Play baseball?" I venture.

"Exactly!" He points at me. "You are the one who deserves credit for this. This morning, you couldn't wait to get out of the house. The sun was out. You are a boy. You wanted to play baseball."

"Um, what do I get credit for?"

"I was stuck in my little world of rain," my dad says. "Rain Redirection Systems require rain, so I didn't mind rain. But rain is wet, Roy. It's wet and bothersome. People would rather have it *not* rain, so they can do stuff. I forgot that people do stuff."

"They do?"

"Baseball. Tennis. Croquet. Boccie ball. Barbecues. Sunbathing. Roy, people here have lost their yards, their tennis courts, their boccie ball courts, their barbecues, their decks and patios. What's more, nobody in town is left to give them those things. Why not me? I have tools, I have staff, and I have materials. It's just a matter of remembering what people do when it doesn't rain."

"So you're going into the tennis court business?"

"Landscaping, small construction projects. Why, I bet I can even use all that plastic for something. Covering swimming pools, maybe. Roy, it's just a matter of matching your business to the weather."

"Sure." I'm glad he's feeling better. My dad is nothing if not an optimist. He really believes everything will turn out well, and he's usually right, except in the kitchen.

"Hey, Dad, I wonder if I can use some of my money. I want to buy grass seed."

"Sure, sure. You know where it is."

"I won't need all of it. Just enough to buy some grass seed."

"Hey, it's your money. Besides, when it doesn't rain, you gotta play baseball, right?"

"Right."

"Tell you what," he says. "I'm heading to the home and garden store in Sutton for some supplies on Monday. Why don't you ride along? You can buy the seed there."

"Sure. That'll be great. I'll even go down and start planting grass when we get back."

"Do you want this chili with water chestnuts? For a little added crunch?"

"However you like it." I hurry to the office before I become any more of an accomplice.

When I open the desk drawer, I see *two* paychecks. One is mine, clean and crisp. The other check is crumpled and creased, made out to Sturgis Nye.

Sunday morning, Sturgis is up, showered, and nicely dressed before I even roll out of bed.

"I hope you don't mind if I use the shoes again," he says. He's already wearing them.

"Not at all. Grandma duty?"

"Just have to get the basket together."

"Watch out for wolves."

Pretty soon the two of them are roaring out of the driveway, and I'm all by myself for another lazy Sunday. I decide to mess around on the computer until the Cubs are on. Today they're playing the Brewers, the other perennial noncontender in the NL Central. It's certainly a can't-miss game.

Speaking of perennial noncontenders, I check my e-mail and find that Adam has been to his game with the Royals. He tells me a very special baseball is on its way to me but won't tell me who signed it. He's attached a couple of digital photographs. One is of him and a Royals pitcher named Mike Wood. The other is of him and his Little League All-Star team sitting in the dugout at what I guess is the Kansas City ballpark.

I reply and find myself writing a pretty long e-mail. I tell him about the sudden lack of rain and the Fourth of July and Rita. I realize again I've avoided talking about Sturgis and wonder why that is. It's not because I don't like him. It's just that I have a hard time describing him, I think.

"I know this kid who's got a heck of an arm," I add to the e-mail at last. "He can't work a curveball, though, so you got nothing to worry about."

Chapter 9

My dad shakes me awake in the morning.

"Did you forget that today was a workday?"

I can't formulate words yet, so I wave at the window, where the sunlight is shining through the blinds, promising another great day. It's a great day I'm not ready to greet. I flop back into bed to sleep for another five or six hours.

"You have to plant a baseball field," my father reminds me. "You're going to cash your check, buy grass seed, and plant the field." He springs the blinds open, flooding the room with hateful sunlight. "You need a baseball field if you want to play baseball."

I wake up a bit and glance at the clock, then wake all the way up, realizing how late it is.

"Five minutes," I tell him, and I'm probably ready in four.

"Is Sturgis coming?" I ask as my father hands me a toasted waffle sandwich (don't ask) and we head out to his truck.

"He went off with Frank," he tells me. "Frank has some work to do and wanted Sturgis to help out."

I don't know what kind of work Frank has to do, but I guess I can't blame him for hiring Sturgis instead of me. He's a better worker, no doubt about that.

There are long lines at the bank, so it's maybe an hour before I can cash my check and get out of there. It's nothing compared to the home and garden store in Sutton, though.

It's mobbed with people from Moundville, buying grills, lawn ornaments, and everything else.

They seem to be out of grass seed, though. All I see is rows of empty pallets.

Despite the crowd, my dad is able to nab a salesman. He's good at stuff like that.

"Can you please help my son?"

"Yeah, of course. Two seconds." The guy finishes unloading a box of stone porcupines.

"I have to pick up a few things, Roy. Be right back." My dad wanders off down the aisle.

"We need grass seed," I tell the salesman when the porcupines are all in order.

"We were cleaned out by yesterday," he says. "We're getting a shipment in later this week, but it'll go fast."

"Can you set some aside for us?"

"I can try. What kind of grass do you want, and how much?"

"We want to seed a baseball field. What kind of seed should we use, and how much do you think it'll take?"

"Well," he says, "a good rule of thumb is ten pounds of seed for every thousand square feet. For sports fields that get a lot of use, you want something like Kentucky bluegrass or rye. Probably a mix. How big is the field?"

I shake my head. "I'm not sure. Regular size, I guess."

"Well, how far is it to the outfield wall?"

"Two hundred feet, maybe," I say with a shrug. I'm embarrassed that I've come so unprepared. "Maybe bigger."

"All right," he says, rolling his eyes up and doing mental math, which I'm sure involves pi and other mysteries. "So that's going to be maybe thirty-six thousand square feet, with some foul territory, right?"

"If you say so," I say.

"Just a ballpark estimate," he says with a wink, and I'm sorry my dad isn't there to enjoy his pun.

"So how much will that cost?" I ask.

"It's 28 bucks a bag." He looks up as he does the math in his head. "So 36 times 28 is . . . Well, you got 28 times 30 and that's 840, plus another 168. . . . Kid, you're looking at at least a thousand bucks."

"Wow" is all I can say. It's going to cost a lot more than I have.

"What do you know about planting a field of that size?"

"Nothing."

"Were you just going to throw handfuls of seed around?"

"Um, sort of."

"Look," he says, "it's not that easy. First you have to level the field. You can use metal rakes for that, if it's not too bad right now, but it's better to use heavy machinery. You also have to make sure there's good drainage, for when it rains." I can't help but laugh, and he stops.

"Sorry, didn't mean to snort at you. It's just that I'm from Moundville."

"Assuming it rains a normal amount, of course," he continues. "You'll need some hoes for that and some aerators and a spreader." He gets me a brochure that explains it all, with

recommended products for greener lawns. Grass seed, fertil-
izer, weed control, insect control. The salesman goes on to
explain the process, and my head spins as the hours and dol-
lars add up in my mind.

"Look that over, and let me know if you have questions,"
the salesman says, and wanders off.

I look glumly at the brochure and get the worst shock
of all.

"Grass will start to grow in seven to fourteen days," says
the small print under the picture of a bag of grass seed.
"Avoid heavy usage for four months."

Four months! That'll be the middle of fall, and that's if
we plant today, which we can't. It'll be next summer before
we can actually play baseball. You hear the expression about
a guy's heart sinking, but you don't know what it means until
it happens to you. My heart sinks right into my stomach,
down through the soles of my feet, and into the hard tile
floor of the store. By the time my dad comes back, it's somewhere around the core of the earth.

"How did it go?" he asks.

"It's impossible," I tell him. I try to recap everything the
salesman told me, but it's a muddle in my head. "It's a lot
more work and money and time than I ever thought," I tell
him as I put the pamphlet in my back pocket.

"Do you wonder why I wanted you and Sturgis to work for
me this summer?" my dad asks me as we drive away from the
store.

I shrug. "Sturgis said we weren't helping that much. He thinks we were just in Frank's way."

"Sturgis said that?"

"Not angry like." I don't want Sturgis to sound like a brat. "He just didn't see that we were making much difference. He still worked hard."

"He's a pretty sharp kid," says my dad. "It's true. I didn't expect you to make much difference. I just thought it would be a good experience for you. You're the same age I was when the rains started. It put my dad out of work. Well, you know what happened."

Yeah, I've heard the stories before about my granddad, even if I never met him. He did landscaping and odd jobs, painted houses, and worked on farms, patching things together to get by. My dad says he worked fourteen-to-sixteen-hour days, sometimes all summer. In the winters, if there was nothing to do, he'd get cabin fever. He'd either hang around the house, drinking and smoking way too much, or go off on road trips and disappear for days. He was a good man when he was busy, my dad says. He just didn't like to be inside and couldn't stand to be idle.

When the rains came, he got really restless. He hated the rain. He liked sunshine and hot days. So after a few months of rain, he took one of his impromptu road trips and never came back. He died in a hotel fire, someplace around St. Louis. He fell asleep with a lit cigarette, probably three sheets to the wind.

As soon as he was old enough, my father dropped out of

school and started working full-time, selling and installing the Rain Redirection Systems. He sometimes says he learned a lot more working than he ever did at school.

School must mean something to him, though, because eventually he earned his degree at a night school in Sutton. That diploma is in his office, dated just a few weeks before I was born. My dad tells me he went into overdrive when my mom was pregnant, driving into Sutton just about every night and going days at a time without sleep, so he could finish up before I was born. He didn't want his son to have a dropout for a dad.

"I thought a job would do you good, like it did for me," he says now. "At first, I thought it would be lonely work, but when Sturgis came, well, it worked out great. You could work and have company. I just didn't expect your lesson to last, what, a few days?"

"Five and a half."

"That's a pretty short lesson," he says. "But it's better than nothing."

"What lesson was I supposed to learn?" I ask. I'm not a big fan of character-building exercises, to be honest.

"Well, you know I want you to be as big a star as you can be," says my dad. "I think you can be a major leaguer, an all-star, even a Hall of Famer. I think you have it in you, and I'll do whatever I can to help."

"I don't know about that." Parents always think their kids can do anything. You can't hit a major-league fastball with your parents' love, though.

"I just don't want you to become a jerk in the process," my dad says. "I knew a guy in high school who went into the majors. Well, he was a jerk anyway, but once he got in the big leagues, he just got worse. When he came back, he thought he was better than the rest of us. Better than guys like me who worked for a living instead of playing a kids' game."

He's never mentioned knowing a major leaguer before. Maybe he's making it up, just to drive his point home.

"Don't be like that, Roy. I knew you were in over your head when you talked about fixing up the old ball field, but I wanted you to find out for yourself. I want you to appreciate the work that goes into getting the field ready. I want you to thank the groundskeepers and sign autographs for their children. Those guys could be your own grandfather. Heck, they could be me. When fans turn out, think about how hard you worked this week and remember they worked that hard all week to take their family to a ball game. Maybe you play a hundred fifty games in a season, but they only get to see the one. Make it worth their while, every time."

"I will, Dad."

He's driving toward home, but he suddenly changes lanes and turns right, toward downtown.

"You're not done learning yet," my dad says.

He pulls over and parks in front of the baseball field. There are a couple of other trucks already parked. I look out onto the field and see Sturgis and Peter working with hoes, spreading fresh soil around, Sturgis working in his quiet way while Peter talks up a storm. The other truck is a flatbed, loaded with fresh sod.

Two guys are unloading the sod onto a big cart, to roll it out into the field. One of them is Frank, although it takes a second to recognize him without his raincoat. The other one is a kid I recognize but can't place right away.

"I sent Frank out yesterday to get soil and sod," my dad explains. "I couldn't wait another year to see a baseball game in Moundville. I've been waiting too long as it is."

I realize who the kid is. I know him from Sutton Little League. Not my team, unfortunately. His real name is Peter Labatte, but most kids in Little League call him the Bat. The Bat gets on base just about every time he comes to the plate, slapping balls all over the field like a junior Ichiro Suzuki, even swinging at balls way out of the zone and hitting them to the gap. He can hit for average, and he has a little power, too. Not necessarily out-of-the-ballpark power but definitely bouncing-it-off-the-fence power. I never called a pitch he didn't hit. I don't know they've invented a pitch he can't hit. I guess that Peter Labatte is Peter's kid. I kind of see the resemblance, now that I know to look for it. Was my dad able to hire him after all? More importantly, will he play for our team?

"We'll need to get this all done today." My dad's voice gets my attention back to the task at hand. "We need to get it all laid down and watered before we go home."

"Dad, how much did this all cost?"

"You don't want to know," he says. "You can pay me back

100

when you're a millionaire ballplayer. Anyway, it's not just for you. It's for my new business."

He points at a huge banner hanging over the outfield fence.

"Field by Moundville Landscaping and Home Improvements," it reads. "Lawns. Pools. Decks. Hot Tubs. Etc." "What Will You Do When the Sun Shines?" it says at the bottom, along with Dad's cell phone number.

"Great idea, Dad."

"Let's get to work!" he says, waving at the piles of fresh-cut sod.

Even with the six of us working, it's a long day. It turns out resodding is even harder than digging. It's all bending and crawling around.

Peter is kind of in charge because he's done this before.

"I set up Little League fields, even a couple of semipro fields," he tells me. "I've been a groundskeeper, batboy, clubhouse manager, umpire. . . . I've done it all. Except play." He holds up his disfigured hand to remind me why.

"That's cool." Maybe I misjudged him. I thought he was a bit weird, but anybody who likes baseball that much has to be okay.

"I'm glad my dad was able to hire your son after all," I tell him, embarrassed because I never actually asked him if he could.

"Technically, he works for me," Peter says. "I'm an independent contractor now."

101

Peter Junior is all over the place, raking the field, dragging out flats of sod, and planting them. It looks like he's done it before, too. He barely talks to anyone as he cuts back and forth, all business.

"I've seen you play," I tell him as we put down the last square of sod. "I've played against you, even."

"You were with the Reds, right?"

"Yeah." His team was the Pirates. They won the play-offs in Sutton and went on to the state championship. They were good. "I was thinking, you should come back and play with us when the field is ready."

"I might," he says, but the way he says it sounds more like a no. We've got the sod in place, and he stalks off before I can ask him any more questions.

I can barely eat one plate of ham and pickle casserole before I drag myself off to my room and collapse on the bed.

Sturgis sacks out, too.

"I never knew it was so much work to have a ballpark."

"Me neither."

"You must have gone to a lot of big-league ballparks when you were a kid."

He shrugs. "Just the one in Baltimore, when I was like two years old."

"I've never been to a big-league park," I admit. "Must be nice. You get to sit up close, see the players? Cal Ripken, maybe?"

"I was more interested in the trains back then. The ball-park in Baltimore is right by the train tracks."

"Yeah, I know."

"I'd get all excited when the trains went by. I'd clap and holler. That's about all I remember."

"Yeah, trains are pretty cool," I agree.

We're up early the next morning. We're aching from the hard work but too excited to stay in bed. We have a quick breakfast of graham cereal and run down to the ballpark. Sturgis is actually just jogging, but I have a hard time keeping up. It's because he has those long legs, like an ostrich or something.

I stop short when we get there. The new grass glistens in the sun, and I want to cry. It's beautiful. There's no mound, no bases, and no batter's box. The bleachers are falling apart. But the outfield is beautiful.

"My dad hates indoor baseball," Sturgis says. "He says Minnesota and Toronto are the worst ballparks in the world. I can see why."

"I like the grass myself," I tell him. "It's all about the grass."

We drop our gear and sprawl out on the new grass, feeling its cool bristles beneath us and squinting against the sunlight. Neither of us says anything more. There's nothing to talk about. For the moment, I'm completely happy. I don't need St. James Academy or Rita or anything else. I drift off into easy sleep, blissful between new grass and a dry sky, with nothing left to dream about.

"This is fantastic!" says Steve. He's come with Tim, Miggy, David, and Kazuo. I wonder where they were yesterday, when we needed their help. Sturgis and I have awoken from our reveries and are casually tossing a ball high into the air, just to watch it fall and bounce on the grass.

David starts running around in circles, his arms out, like a little kid playing airplane. Kazuo just drops to his knees and fans his hand through the grass, then looks up at me with a mixture of disbelief and joy.

"Can we play on it?" he asks.

"In a couple of days," I tell him. "Maybe even tomorrow. Just take it easy on the grass today."

"We need to get a team together and play baseball," says Steve.

"Well, we need a mound," I remind him. "We need to put down a better surface in the infield, and we need bases."

"Ah, we can get all that," he says with a wave of his hand, as if it's nothing. I remember how he said the turf was "a little grass and some dirt." Steve takes all that stuff for granted.

"Let's get a team together and get one of those traveling teams to come play us," says Miggy. "It would be beautiful, man."

"Oh yeah," says Steve. "Bring it on!"

"We should replay that one game," says Sturgis.

"You mean against Sinister Bend? They don't really exist anymore," I remind him.

"There's always a they," he says. "It's a fact of life."

"I don't know," I say. I like the idea in theory, but you can't play baseball against a bunch of ghosts unless you're Kevin Costner.

"Maybe Moundville could finally win that way," Steve offers. "Sinister Bend will have to forfeit because they don't exist."

"Yeah!" Miggy and some of the other kids laugh.

"Never mind Sinister Bend. If I could get someone to play us," asks Sturgis, "would you guys all play? Hypothetically, I mean."

"Sure," says Steve.

"Of course," I agree.

Kazuo looks less sure. "It sounds like fun, but we barely know how to play."

"These guys will teach you," says Sturgis, waving his hand at me and Steve. "They know the game inside and out."

I think aloud, wondering what our chances are against an average team. "Sturgis has a great arm. We won't need to score a lot of runs to win." Sturgis pretends to be humble, but I catch a look in Steve's eye. "Steve's a great player, too," I add. "He's got a lot of power for a middle infielder." That perks him up.

"I've always wanted to play in a real game," says Kazuo. "Can I play shortstop?"

That's Steve's favorite position, but he doesn't object. "I'll play second," he says.

Kazuo runs out to a spot between first and second base, pretending to field balls and pivot.

"That's second," I call out.

"What?"

"You're supposed to be over there." I point between second and third base.

"Really?" He looks confused.

"Why don't you play there, and I'll play over here," says Steve, trotting out to his usual shortstop position.

"But I'm still the shortstop, right?" Kazuo asks.

"Sure," says Steve. "We'll just play it this way."

"Excellent," says Kazuo. So we have an ambidextrous switch-hitting shortstop who doesn't know left from right playing second base. He looks happy, though, so who am I to complain?

"What about me?" asks David.

"You'll be our left fielder," I decide. He's a runty kid, and I don't put much faith in his fielding. He'll do the least damage in left field, especially if I shade the center fielder that way. Once I find a center fielder, that is.

Sturgis stands where the mound ought to be, and I trot back behind where the plate ought to be. I scan the field and think about kids I know, mentally filling in the gaps.

"I think we can do it," I say to Sturgis. "Just get us a them."

Chapter 10

Our first real practice is scheduled for Thursday, giving the grass time to get its roots down deep. I'm so excited I head out about an hour early. As I'm walking to the ballpark, a fat raindrop splashes down in front of me. I stop and look up, hoping it's just my imagination. A second drop plops in my eye, and a third smacks my forehead.

A moment later, I'm in the middle of an all-out downpour. I run on ahead to the ballpark, seeking refuge in the dugout. My dad has re-covered the overhang with surplus plastic, of which he has plenty, so it's pretty dry in there.

When I duck in, I see that Kazuo is already there, waiting. He nods at me solemnly.

"It's just a regular rain," he says.

"I hope you're right." I try to figure out the percentages, but there are too many variables to think about.

"Why are you here so early?" he asks. "Practice isn't for another hour."

"I just like the empty ballpark."

"Me too."

We sit in silence for a while and watch the rain.

"You can sort of make pictures out of the raindrops," Kazuo says at last.

"Yeah, like I never played that game before," I tell him. We both laugh. Kids in Moundville have all done their share of rain watching.

The rain lightens up after about a half hour. We step out of the dugout, onto the silvery grass, and look at the sky as the clouds hurry away to ruin someone else's day.

"I told you," he says. "It was just a regular rain."

"I believed you."

"I believed me, too, but I'm still relieved."

The next one to arrive is Peter Junior. He just drifts in, like he didn't really mean to wind up here, in particular, but just sort of found himself here. He's been caught in the rain but doesn't seem to care that he's soaked.

"Hey, Peter."

"You can call me P.J.," he says. "My dad is doing an odd job in town. Garage door. I thought I'd come see how the field was doing."

"You want to play?" I toss him the ball. He catches it easily but doesn't toss it back right away.

"I'm already on a baseball team," he says apologetically. "The Pirates, remember?"

"I'm just talking about practice."

"I guess I can hang around for a while."

Steve brings a couple of new players with him: Anthony and Miggy's kid brother Carlos. They even bring gloves, so we're able to fill in the infield and run some drills. We just take turns at the plate, the rest of us trying different spots in the field.

We hardly even need anyone in the outfield with Sturgis pitching. He smokes those balls in there, and he has scary

108

control. He puts the ball wherever I put my glove. It's the best anyone can do just to tap the ball back into the infield. Except for P.J., that is.

P.J. doesn't spend too much time in the infield. He'd rather bat and keeps sneaking back into the box, way out of turn. He grounds out the first couple of times, but once he figures out Sturgis's fastball, he starts lining base hits left and right.

I think he should show the rest of us how he does it, but his dad drives up and beeps the horn to go home.

"See you around," I tell him as he sprints off.

"Maybe," he calls back.

Without P.J., Sturgis is able to cruise past us. It would probably be better to have someone else pitch for a while and let the guys work on their swings, but I'm too stunned by Sturgis to make him stop. It's just fascinating to watch. He proves to be as tireless as he is effective, striking out one batter after another without slowing down.

A pitcher is only as good as his defense, though, and our defense is terrible. For instance, when Tim grounds a ball to short, Miggy charges it from his spot at third base and fights Steve over it.

"It's not a contest," I yell at him. "Know your territory and field it."

A few seconds later, David is playing third and Miggy is batting. He squibs it to Sturgis, who picks it up and tosses it to . . . well, to nobody. There's nobody there. Anthony is playing first base, but he's nowhere near the base.

"Can I get a little help here?" Sturgis asks.

"I thought you had it," says Anthony with a shrug.

"I guess I'll just have to strike everyone out," Sturgis grumbles.

Anthony takes a turn at catcher while I bat. Sturgis does strike me out, but Anthony lets strike three skip off his glove, and I run safely to first.

Sturgis throws his glove to the ground. "Can you guys maybe get an out once in a while?" he asks.

"Hey, we're just practicing," says David. "Take it easy, Scarface."

Sturgis makes a move at him, but Steve stops him.

"Why don't you take your turn at the plate," says Sturgis to David, trying to pull away from Steve. "I'll throw the baseball right through your chest, you little maggot."

"Chill!" says Anthony.

"Team meeting," I holler, coming off first and waving everybody in.

David rolls his eyes at me, but Anthony kind of gives him a look that says, "Cool it," and he does. We huddle around where the mound ought to be.

"First off," I say, "no more throwing beanballs or names." I remember how authoritatively Frank said practically those same words at the work site, but I don't get the same results.

"You ain't the boss of me," Anthony grumbles.

"What are you going to do about it anyway?" David wants to know.

"Kick you off the team."

"It's not *your* team," he says. "It's not even *a* team, really."

"Second of all," I continue, "Sturgis is right. You aren't really practicing. You're just waiting for your turn to bat and not trying to play defense." I think P.J. set a bad example when he was here.

Miggy shakes his head, and Carlos shakes his head in imitation.

"Who died and made you coach?" David complains.

"He's not the coach, he's the team captain," says Steve.

"Since when?"

"Since he should be."

"For one thing, he actually knows how to play the game," says Sturgis.

"I know how to play, too," David mutters. "It's not that hard."

"Let's vote," says Kazuo seriously. "Baseball captains should be elected by the team."

"He's right," I agree.

"I'll nominate him," says Steve.

"Me too," says Sturgis. "What's more, if you nimrods don't vote for him, I'm walking off right now."

"I nominate nobody." David kicks at the infield dirt. "I don't want a captain."

"Me too," says Miggy. "I just want to have fun, not get bossed around."

"Me too," says Carlos.

"All in favor of Roy as captain?" asks Steve.

I don't like to vote for myself, but I know the numbers. I

raise my hand, and so do Steve, Sturgis, and Kazuo. David glares at Kazuo, who's supposed to be his best friend.

"I just want us to be good," Kazuo explains.

"All opposed?" Steve asks. David raises his hand, and so do Miggy and Carlos. Slowly, Anthony raises his own hand in agreement.

"I guess we don't have a captain," says David. "It's a tie. You need a majority." At first I wish P.J. were still around to break the tie, but then, he'd probably vote against me.

"This is stupid," says Sturgis. "Go form your own team, you little snots. We don't need you dragging us down anyway."

"Take it easy, Sturgis," I say. I don't want the team to break up before we even have a full practice.

"Hey," says Steve, pointing. "We have some new players."

"Girls." David rolls his eyes.

That tall girl with brown hair I saw at the gym and again on the Fourth of July is walking across the field, carrying a new glove. With her—a little bit behind her, so I don't see her at first—is Rita. I feel a thrill go through me. She's even cuter than I remember.

"I heard you were getting a baseball team together," says the tall girl.

I suddenly realize why she looks familiar. I've seen her on TV. She won some state tennis thing this spring.

"You're Shannon, right?"

"Right. We were wondering if you need any more players."

"Actually, we could use a good center fielder." I think about how she ran all over the tennis court, getting to everything, and my hopes for the defense pick up.

"I'm Rita," Rita tells me, not knowing I've had her name bouncing around in my head for the last two weeks. "I've never played baseball," she says apologetically. "I'd like to try, though."

"She's a good tennis player, too," Shannon adds.

"Says the girl who currently has an eighty-to-one record against me!" Rita protests.

"Hey, you beat me once," says Shannon. "That's more than my brother can say."

"We're happy to give you a tryout," I tell them, or mean to say, but I think I switch a couple of words around. "By the way, I'm Roy," I add (or maybe "By the Roy, I'm way"), and I go around the mound to introduce everyone else.

"Hey," Steve asks them, "how do you feel about Roy here as captain of the team?"

"Sure," says Rita.

"Okay with me," says Shannon.

"Ha!" Sturgis pumps his fist. "Motion carries."

David's face falls. "I don't think their votes should count," he says. "They came in after we already voted."

"So we'll just call another vote," says Steve.

"I change my vote anyway," says Anthony. "I want Roy to be captain."

"Me too," says Miggy.

"Yeah," says Carlos.

"Fine," says David, sighing in exasperation.

"Thanks," I say. "I won't make a victory speech. Let's just take a break, then practice some more."

"Thanks for your help," I tell Sturgis when we break huddle.

He shrugs it off like it's nothing. "We need someone to be in charge. Better you than some old guy making us run laps."

"What makes you think I won't make you run laps?"

"'Cause you'd have to run them, too?"

"Oh, right."

"Seriously," he says, almost in a whisper, "I want us to be good. That's all."

"I wonder why Anthony changed his mind so fast?"

He laughs. "That girl. Shannon is, like, really beautiful. Anthony didn't care if you were captain or not. He just knew he was on her side, whatever it was."

"Oh yeah?" I check out Shannon again and can see that, yeah, she's a bit of a knockout, if that's your type. I can also see that Anthony is hovering around her, making small talk, trying to demonstrate what he knows about baseball.

"Well, he seems to have a lot of pull with the other guys," I say. "I'm glad he changed his mind."

"You crack me up," he says. "You see that girl walk out here, and you just think about where to put her in the outfield." He lets out a long breath and shakes his head. "Man, that's focus if I ever saw it. You so need to be captain of this team."

"Yeah, well, I'm kind of . . ." I don't finish the sentence because some of the other guys are walking by. I see a flicker of recognition in his face, though, when he realizes that Rita is *my* Rita.

We run some fielding drills I know from camp. We aren't much better at the end of practice, but at least everyone is trying.

The funny thing is, David is a pretty good player. He can read the ball right off the bat and makes clean catches. He can't throw hard, but he throws straight.

"Hey, David," I say, "let me see your glove."

He passes it to me with a curious look on his face.

"It's not too used. See if you can still return it."

"Oh, shut up!" he says. "I don't want to play on your stupid team anyway. Not if you're captain!"

He sprints off, and I have to chase him. He's fast, too, I think. Probably be a good base stealer.

"Wait!" I holler.

He gets winded pretty quickly, and I'm able to grab his shirt and spin him around.

"You need to listen," I tell him, panting. "I'm not kicking you off the team. I just want you to trade this glove for one of the really big ones. You might have seen the ones where the fingers look like a shovel?"

"Sure," he says, looking at me skeptically.

"Those are first baseman's gloves. Get one of those. I want you to play first base."

"You're trying to stick me at first base? I thought I got to play left field!"

"First base is the most important position, after the pitcher. You make eighty percent of the outs." I have no idea if this is true, but it sounds good.

"Really?"

"Sure. Think about it. If you want to stay in the outfield, stay in the outfield. But if you want to play first, get a first baseman's glove before that one's beat up."

"Okay. Hey, if a pitcher is most important and a first baseman is second most important, what's the catcher?"

"The catcher is even more important than the pitcher. Without the catcher, the pitcher's nothing."

Chapter 11

I get my signed baseball from Adam in the mail, and it comes with a letter of explanation.

"Well, Roy," it begins, "I really wanted to get you a signed ball. I brought three baseballs to the game with me, knowing we'd get to hang out in the dugout before the game. I had one for me, one for my little brother, and one for you.

"As you know, the Royals have a catcher named John Buck, and he's no great shakes, but I thought he'd sign your ball. I couldn't find him, though, so I asked this bench coach, 'Hey, where's John Buck?' and he said, 'He's in the bullpen warming up the pitcher.' So I handed the guy your ball and asked him if he could go get Buck to sign it. I didn't care as much if he signed mine, since I had basically no room left for signatures after Graffanino and Grudzielanek and Mientkiewicz all signed it. Roy, when those guys turn a double play, the announcers usually take a commercial break in the middle of the call."

I snicker as I flip the page over to read the back. I realize I miss Adam's sense of humor.

"Anyway, I gave the ball to the bench coach, and he gave it to a batboy, and that kid ran off to the clubhouse, even though John Buck was right over in the bullpen warming up Mike Wood (who stank to the tune of eight earned runs in four-plus innings, by the way).

"We weren't allowed to hang out in the dugout much

longer. They had good seats for us, but not on the bench, so I needed to get your ball back quick. So I asked another bat-boy about it, and he ran off to find the first batboy. Just as we were getting herded up and made to leave, the second kid ran back and handed me the ball.

"I glanced at it and it looked wrong, so I asked him what was up, and he said, 'It's signed by Buck liked you asked for,' but it said 'John "Buck" O'Neil,' not 'John Buck.' We were shuttled off to our seats before I could get an explanation."

I shake my head in embarrassment, because Adam doesn't know who Buck O'Neil was, and keep reading.

"All during the top half of the first inning, I just turned that ball over and over, looking at it. My coach saw it, and his jaw dropped open.

"'Don't you know who that is?' he asked me.

"'Nope,' I told him.

"So he told me that Buck O'Neil played for the Kansas City Monarchs, and that he was the Negro Leagues' batting champion a couple of times, and that he managed the team for years, and knew Jackie Robinson and signed Ernie Banks, and wound up being the first black coach in baseball. Buck's a local legend, he said, and one of the finest men ever to wear a baseball uniform. You can bet I looked him up later on the Web, and, wow, that was some misunderstanding the batboy made. You had a gem of a ball waiting for you, Roy.

"The only problem was, the coach was all choked up, talking about Buck O'Neil and the KC Monarchs and every-thing. He went on to tell me about how his grandfather played in the Negro Leagues and everything Buck O'Neil has done to celebrate the history of those leagues and promote the Negro Leagues HOF. Mr. Daniels is a good guy, Roy. He's a barber most of the time, but he's also a pretty good coach.

"Long story short, I told Coach to keep that baseball, and I got another ball signed for you.

"Best wishes, Adam.

"P.S. The Royals were playing the Cards. I got Pujols to sign a ball for my bro. He just about exploded. My brother, I mean. Pujols didn't explode."

My ball is signed by Montgomery Daniels, full-time barber and part-time baseball coach. I'm pretty happy with it and place it among my trophies and memorabilia.

After a dinner of spinach surprise (the surprise part is Vienna sausages), Sturgis wants to practice his pitching.

"Teach me that junkball again," he says.

"I thought you didn't like it."

"A couple of you guys nearly got decent hits," he says. "I need to be better."

We go out in the yard and toss the ball back and forth. I show him how to hold the ball again, with the extra finger to slow it down.

He tries a few. They're slow enough, but they don't look much like fastballs.

"That's all?" he says. "Anyone can do that."

"You're not doing it," I tell him. "You step off the wrong

way and throw differently. I can see it coming a mile off. It has to be the same as your fastball or it's no good."

"I am doing it the same," he protests.

"No you're not," I tell him. "I have another idea. Instead of using your finger to slow down the pitch, try just holding the ball further back in your hand."

He looks at me strangely and then throws a perfectly good change-of-pace pitch at me.

"Like that?"

"Yes!"

"What's the big deal about that? That isn't hard."

I just shake my head and make him throw some more. He's got it working, all right. He couldn't figure out the three-finger changeup, but he's got big hands that are perfect for the palmball.

"Let's call your fastest pitch a ten. Throw me a ten."

He rears back and throws. The ball stings my hand.

"Now throw me that cookie."

He does, and a pretty slow pitch pops into my glove. It looks okay, sort of like a fastball, but there's no zip on it.

"Try something right in between. Edge the ball back a bit in your hand."

He throws the hard one, then the soft one, and can't seem to find anything in between. I can see he's getting annoyed.

"It just takes practice," I tell him. I toss the ball back. He tries a few more, with different grips, until he can throw a nice in-betweener.

"We'll call that one a five. Throw it again."

He finds that grip again a few pitches later and then throws three good ones, right in a row. He's a quick learner.

"Now throw the ten again."

He rears back and throws wild.

"Darn it," he says, punching his glove.

"That's what makes pitching hard." I find the ball in a bunch of weeds that have all of a sudden sprung up near the back steps. "Being able to throw any pitch at any time. It just takes lots of practice."

"Maybe we can practice every evening, after dinner?" he asks.

"Um, sure." Day practices and evening drills are a lot of baseball, even for me, but I want Sturgis to master the changeup.

"My dad hated junkball pitching. If he knew I was throwing junkballs, he'd kill me."

I shrug. "You can't get by on one pitch," I tell him. "The fastball is only good for a few outs. Eventually, batters catch up to it and you're dead meat. You need another pitch."

"That explains my dad's career, right there," he says.

My dad gets the town to put up some money for materials for the ballpark, promising to match with in-kind contribution, which means his crew will do the work for free. His crew being Sturgis and me, for the most part.

He can't even help that much himself because he has a new job.

121

"Remember the home and garden store in Sutton?" he asks.

"Yeah, sure."

"I'm the new manager in the lumber section. I start Monday."

"Wow. That's cool, I guess." It's hard to imagine my dad taking orders from someone else.

"Just until business picks up," he says. "Hey, I also get an employee discount. That'll come in handy."

Among the great ironies of all times, Moundville is now having a minor drought. Sturgis and I have to go out early every day to water and tend to the field. My dad pays Peter to mow every third day, spinning around on one of those riding mowers. Sometimes P.J. gets to ride it, but never me or Sturgis. We just do the grunt work.

When we see P.J., I ask him to take a few swings against Sturgis.

"I don't know," he says. "I'm supposed to be helping my dad."

"Just take a few swings," I tell him, handing him a bat.

It's a dirty trick. I know that once he's got a bat in his hand, he's going to want to swing it. Sturgis serves him nothing but flame and smoke, and eventually P.J. always catches up to it. Once he does, it's all over. Every pitch is jolted into the outfield, some of them rattling the wire fence. It seems like it would be stuff for a good rivalry, but Sturgis just tips his hat whenever a pitch is walloped.

"We have to get him on our team," he tells me.

"What do you think I'm trying to do?"

One Saturday, maybe two weeks after laying down the sod, we're back to shoveling. I didn't miss it one bit, but it's for a good cause, making way for a new diamond. We put down good infield dirt, real bases and a plate, and replace the backstop. We paint the white lines that mark off the baselines and install a pitcher's mound. With the three of us and the two Peters, we do it all in a day.

My dad has also bought about a half dozen bats, a bag of balls, and other supplies, and a surprise for Sturgis. He just tosses it to him, like it's nothing. It's a brand-new mitt, big enough for Sturgis's large hands. He slides his hand in and flexes it in the stiff new leather.

"It feels weird," he says.

"You just have to break it in," I tell him. "You need to oil it a bit and use it for a few weeks."

"Yeah, I know."

Sturgis goes out on the new mound and stamps around a bit and takes a few warm-up tosses. His new glove fits him perfectly. Like a glove, in fact.

"It's a lot better up there, isn't it?" I ask.

He just nods.

He looks at my dad. "Um," he croaks. The words die before they can find their way out of his mouth. He just looks down at the new mound and punches the glove a couple of times.

"It's nothing," says my dad.

My mom calls the same day, wondering if it's started raining yet. She sounds pretty sober, but rushed. In between flights or something. I tell her about the new infield.

"Dad made it all happen," I tell her.

"He knows how to cut a deal," she says. "Hey, how's Sturgis?"

"He's fine," I tell her. "Hey, how do you know about Sturgis?" My dad hardly talks to her, and I don't remember mentioning it myself. She blathers about running into so-and-so on a flight she was working and catching up on the latest Moundville gossip.

"Does Sturgis play baseball, too?" she asks.

"Oh yeah. He's a pretty good pitcher."

"Of course he is," she says. "Like father, like son."

"You know about his dad?"

"He was a big leaguer, Roy."

"Yeah, I know. I guess I'm just surprised you knew about that." I wonder if I like it better when she's a little drunk and nonsensical or cold sober and creepy and knowing.

"Tell him I said hi," she says. We say we love each other, and she's off to fly to wherever she's going. I might find out when I get a postcard.

"My mom says hi," I tell Sturgis later.

"That was nice of her," he says.

We now have enough players to field a team, even though one is Miggy's kid brother. Tim can run down fly balls pretty well, so I put him in right field. Rita is another story. She's terrible in the field. She can hit a ball okay, on account of her tennis experience, but she couldn't catch a cold. I figure I'll just have to use her as a pinch hitter—until she tosses me the ball. The ball comes right at my chest, then drops into the dirt.

"Sorry, Captain! I hurt my elbow once playing tennis. I've never been able to throw right since."

"Do that again." I toss the ball back to her. She throws it again, the same way. It's amazing. The ball soars straight at me, then just drops out of the air like a narcoleptic bird.

"Hey, Sturgis, watch. Throw it to him," I tell Rita, tossing the ball back. She does, and Sturgis reaches out for it, just to have it die in front of his glove.

"Pretty good junkball," he says respectfully.

"It's not a junkball, it's a backwards curveball," I tell him. "It comes in on you instead of tailing away. It's called a screwball. Practically nobody can throw it. Rita throws it perfectly, though. It breaks hard."

"Really?" she asks.

"I think you'll be pretty good out of the bullpen," I tell her. I like the idea of having Sturgis throw heat, then having Rita come out with her screwball.

"Between the two of you, I think we can beat anyone."

"Thanks, Captain!" she says. Did I mention it kills me when she calls me Captain?

Toward the end of practice, I look up and see P.J. kind of loitering by the margin of the field.

"Want to grab a bat and take a few swings?" I call over.

Usually I have to plead with him. This time he sprints over. Maybe watching us all flail at pitches has made him eager to show us how it's done.

He does, too. Sturgis throws a few hard fastballs, and P.J. sails them into the outfield. It's about time our outfielders got some practice.

"Let me try," says Rita. She throws a few pitches, and P.J. swings right over them, turning himself around.

"You pitch good!" he says. Rita smiles, and her eyes twinkle a bit, and I resist an urge to take the bat from P.J. and knock him silly.

"Show me that screwball," Sturgis asks that evening. We're in the yard, tossing the ball around.

"Let's just practice the changeup."

He frowns and throws a couple of lazy off-speed pitches. "I get it now. I want to learn that screwball. Or at least a curveball."

"Sturgis, you throw really hard. You work in a good changeup, nobody will be able to hit you. You don't need a curveball."

"Why don't you pitch?" he asks. "You seem to know so much."

"I did pitch a little, back when I played in Sutton, but I guess I like catching better. Anyway, I want to play every day. I've missed too much baseball to sit in the dugout four days out of five or wait around in the bullpen to pitch one or two innings."

"Makes sense."

"Throw me a five."

He tries but delivers a regular fastball.

"Try counting," I suggest as I toss it back. "You know, count from one to whatever pitch you want to throw and imagine the pitch gaining speed as you count. Then let 'er fly."

We work our way up from one to ten that way, with Sturgis counting each time and adding a bit more Tabasco to each pitch.

"Throw me a five," I say after we've been through the drill a couple of times.

He counts to five and throws a good off-speed pitch.

"Now throw me a seven."

He fires again. It's a bit faster than the first, but still not full speed.

"How about a ten?"

He rears back and lets go. I brace myself for the sting, and a second later a marshmallow pops into my glove. He's thrown a perfect changeup. It looked like a fastball and just lost speed on its way to my glove. It was a thing of beauty. The best hitters in the world would swing through a changeup like that.

"I told you, I got the junkball figured out," he says. "Now I want to learn that screwball."

"You'll strike a lot of guys out without a screwball," I tell him. "I'm just glad I won't have to hit your pitching."

I'm feeling okay about our team. We have a pretty good battery in me and Sturgis, and we have Rita if Sturgis gets tired or runs into trouble. Sure, we don't have anything like a pitching rotation, but we can field a strong team for one day, which is all we have to do, if we ever have an opponent.

Our defense is improving, too. Kazuo is solid at second base—when he throws to the right base anyway—and Steve is excellent at shortstop. David is getting good at first base, scooping balls out of the dirt and snatching them out of the air. Shannon is Torii Hunter out there in center field, and Tim does okay in right field.

Our problems are down the third base line. Miggy's at third and is always getting in Steve's way. Carlos is in left field. He's ten years old and can't throw a ball back to the infield without bouncing it a couple of times. I try putting Anthony out there, but he tends to watch Shannon instead of the infield. Rita has her trick pitch but can't throw straight, so she's useless in the field. I feel like we're close, though.

"If we just had any offense at all," I tell Steve after practice one afternoon.

"We have me," he says. "We have you."

"Yeah, well . . ." We're both all right at the plate, but we don't have anyone who would really scare a pitcher. Not the way P.J. does.

"What would it take to get P.J. on board?" I ask.

"He might be thinking about it. Did you see how he gets on with Rita?"

"What?"

"I think they dig each other. See, check it out." He points out the dugout at the field. Sure enough, there's Rita, and there's P.J. Where did he come from? I wonder. They're just making small talk and whatever. The kind of thing I'm no good at.

"On the other hand," I say, "I wouldn't want to quit the Pirates if I was him."

Steve might be right. P.J. shows up the next day wearing workout clothes and carrying his own glove.

"Where do you want me, Captain?" It's not as cute when he says it.

"I guess we could use a left fielder."

"Right," he says. "I mean left."

I'm almost relieved that P.J. is a liability in the outfield. There's a reason he's called the Bat and not the Mitt. I have Steve pitch for a while so we can get good swings and knock the ball around, while the fielders practice running them down. Carlos can't catch anything, but he's usually close enough to have a try. P.J. can't get a good read on a ball, though, and is oftener than not twenty feet away when it falls.

He can't throw either. He throws left-handed, just like he

bats, but I wonder if he shouldn't try throwing with his right hand. I don't know that it would be any weaker or clumsier than his left.

"When do the outfielders get to bat?" Shannon hollers from the outfield.

"I guess now," I holler back. Maybe I let the fielding practice run a little long since P.J. looked so bad doing it.

"Are we ever going to play a real game?" P.J. asks after practice. So it's already "we." I guess that means he's joining the team, but I'm not as thrilled as I thought I'd be. Not just because he seems to like Rita but because there's no designated-hitter rule in youth baseball.

We're done practicing, but everyone is still hanging around, catching their breath. It's about ninety degrees, and we're all a bit spent.

"A real game would be cool," I agree. "It'll be good to see how we do."

"I think we'll get slaughtered," says Steve, "but I want to see how bad."

"I think we should play SJA," says Sturgis.

"St. James Academy?" Steve looks at him in disbelief. "For one thing, that's a high school."

"JV, I mean," Sturgis explains.

"They're still older than us," says Steve. "Besides, school's not even in session."

"They have these clinics throughout the summer," I tell

him. I know St. James's athletic schedule by heart. "But you're right. They're still going to be older than us."

"So?" Sturgis shrugs.

"So they won't want to play us, and even if they do, they'll destroy us. I don't mind us losing a game, but we don't need to be humiliated in the process."

"Well," he says, "they do want to play us. We already set it up."

"What? Who's we?"

"My dad," says P.J. "He talked to their coach on the phone. He said we were a new team in Moundville and just wanted to scrimmage. They want to host us. They need scrimmages, too. They're having a clinic this weekend, it turns out."

"Your *dad* talked to St. James?"

"Sturgis asked him to set it up. We figured it was your idea."

"Sturge?" I look over at him, but he pretends to be so involved with his shoelaces he doesn't notice anything is going on.

"My dad knows the coaches, is all," P.J. explains. "He coaches the Pirates, and some of those guys end up at St. James."

"Well, did he tell his coach buddies how old we are?"

"Not exactly," he says. "Anyway, we're going to scrimmage this Saturday, at their stadium."

"How are we even going to get there?" I ask.

"My dad will drive," says P.J. "That is, if you guys want to play. We can always back out."

"Heck, *I* want to play," says David.

"Me too," says Steve. "My dad will love this. He went to St. James."

"Let's say no parents this time," I say. "Except your dad." I nod at P.J.

"Yeah," says Kazuo. "Otherwise, they'll see how bad we are."

Even Steve sees my point. "My parents cost me an error at the Camp Classic," he remembers. "They were hollering at me to catch the ball, and it kind of distracted me."

"Yeah, I remember that." It was me that scored a run on that error.

When I finally ask who's in, there's no need to count hands. There's hoots and hollers and hats thrown in the air, and it's clear the game is on.

Chapter 12

Peter shows up early Saturday in his old, beat-up truck. P.J. is riding shotgun.

"Are we even going to fit in that thing?" David wants to know.

Peter clambers out to open the back door. "My son's team has ridden in it. It's tight, but you just kind of squish together."

We let Shannon and Rita ride in the cabin, and the rest of us pile into the back, sitting on the hard metal floor, with no air-conditioning and no windows. I bet the Pirates ride like that across town, not twenty miles.

"Remind me why we didn't get rides from our folks?" Steve asks, probably thinking about the surround-sound stereo and comfy seats of his dad's SUV.

"You're sitting on my hand," says P.J. It's not much of an answer, but it's the only one Steve gets.

It is a hot and stuffy ride, but we survive. When we pull in the parking lot behind the St. James baseball field, one of their assistant coaches comes out, telling Peter to move the truck. He's startled when we come scrambling out of the back.

"What? You don't mean to tell me . . . ?" He shouts over the brick wall at someone, and soon the St. James Academy coach and a couple of their players come out to see what's going on. I've met the coach, when my dad and I looked at the school, but I don't think he remembers me.

"Hey, Phil!" Peter slams the back door to the truck and makes his way around to shake the coach's hand.

"Sorry," says the assistant coach. "I didn't realize this was your team . . . um, vehicle."

"The regular team bus is in the shop," Peter jokes.

"You have got to be kidding me," says one of the kids as soon as he sees us. He has hair so blond it's nearly white. He looks to be about fifteen years old. We're in way over our heads.

"On the phone, you made me think you were high school kids." The coach frowns. "We can't play you guys."

"We just want to play the best team around, and that's you," I tell him. The coach definitely doesn't remember me, I decide. When I was here with my dad, he said I was exactly the kind of young man St. James was looking for. Now he can't even look *at* me, let alone *for* me.

"It's just a friendly game," Peter says with a fake-looking smile. "No big deal."

The two coaches whisper between themselves, shaking their heads.

"What happened to your face?" the blond kid asks Sturgis.

Sturgis doesn't answer.

"Hey, ugly, I'm talking to you!"

Sturgis still doesn't speak but kicks at the ground with his sneaker. His scars become starker as his face flushes.

"What happened to *your* face?" David asks the older boy.

"Was your mother scared by a giant *butt* when she was pregnant?"

The coaches break huddle. The assistant says something quietly to the blond boy, who saunters back through the gate.

"The boys are taking a vote," the coach says. "They may not want to play."

"Why not?" asks Sturgis.

"It isn't fair to either one of us. You'll get humiliated, and we'll be called bullies for beating you."

"What if we win?" asks Sturgis.

The coach just laughs. "Well, that's not going to happen, but hypothetically, it would make us a laughingstock. See? It's a no-win situation for us. Either we're seen as bullies or we're seen as losers."

"It's just a scrimmage game," says Peter. "It's not like anyone's even here."

"We get a lot of visitors," he says importantly. "Scouts, the media. You have no idea."

The blond boy returns, grinning. "We voted not to play you kids. It was unanimous."

I'm sure we didn't get a fair vote. He probably made us sound like second graders.

"Chickens!" David stamps his foot. I hope he doesn't start making cluck-cluck noises and flapping his arms, or it's going to be really hard to convince them we're *not* second graders.

"I have an idea," says Sturgis. "How about you give us

one run and try to score two against us? We won't even bat. If you score two runs, you win."

"How many innings?" the coach asks.

"Three innings," says Sturgis coolly. "Once through the lineup."

"It'll still be a slaughter," says the coach.

"We'll quit after you score the second run," says Sturgis. "You can't slaughter us. Nobody can say you did."

"What's the point?" The coach shrugs. "What's in it for us?"

"You really want to see this young man pitch," Peter says. I can't remember if Peter has seen Sturgis pitch, but P.J. might have told him how good Sturgis is. "Better to see him now than when he's pitching against you in a year or two."

"He's that good, huh?"

"The best I've seen, for his age." I guess both coaches know Peter's taken his teams to the Little League World Series a couple of times.

"We can still get a full practice in," says the assistant.

"What the heck," the coach says. "Let's go ask the guys."

The St. James Academy kids are only a couple of years older than us. They might as well be the New York Yankees, though. They look as big and confident as Murderers' Row. They even have pinstripes on their uniforms. Peter says hello to a couple of them and shakes their hands. Those must be the former Pirates.

The coach explains the rules of the scrimmage, and they all like the idea. The blond kid is the only one who votes against it.

"We'll score two quick runs and be over with it," says one of the St. James players. He looks familiar, and I realize why. He looks like his brother, who's been drafted by the Cincinnati Reds and is tearing his way through the minors. The newspapers have regular updates on his progress.

"Put our run on the scoreboard," says Sturgis.

The assistant coach disappears, and soon the visitors' board shows a 1 for the top of the first inning.

"Let's play ball!" the coach shouts.

"I think I'll keep you on the bench," I tell P.J., who's about to trot out to left field. Since we don't get to bat, there's not much point to having him on the team.

"Okay," he says, a bit too cheerfully. I realize when everyone else is in place that I've stupidly left him on the bench with Rita, where he can flirt shamelessly. I feel helpless.

The assistant coach returns with umpire's gear, to call strikes and balls.

"You'll give us a fair strike zone?" I ask him as I take my spot behind the plate.

"Don't test me, boy."

I crouch down and take about a dozen warm-up tosses from Sturgis. I see Miggy and little Carlos off to the left and take a deep breath. We'll have to pitch really aggressively to the right-handed batters, I think.

I smirk behind my mask when I realize Sturgis is throwing all medium stuff to warm up, pretending it's his fastball. He's setting them up. He has the instincts of a poker hustler.

I'm all the happier to see the leadoff hitter is the snotty kid from the parking lot.

I show one finger, then flash five twice, telling Sturgis to bring on the ten.

Sturgis flares his nostrils, takes a deep breath, and brings it. The blond kid jumps back, feigning alarm.

"That nearly hit me!"

"That was a strike, Ned," says the umpire, "right in the zone." That gets the whole St. James team laughing, and Ned turns red.

"Throw that again, brat," he says.

Why not? I show one finger, then flash five twice, then one. I'm calling for the "eleven" pitch, a pitch a mite faster than even his regular fastball. Sturgis can't throw more than a few of those in a game, but this is a good time for it.

Ned readies himself to swing, and the ball comes in with a zip and a bang. He's caught looking again. His jaw drops, and there's a smattering of applause from his teammates.

"Strike two!" The umpire is getting into it now. I think he enjoys seeing Ned look foolish.

"Now really bring it!" I shout at Sturgis. I wiggle my fingers, then flash five. Sturgis takes a quick breath, rears back, and fires. Ned takes a huge swing and turns himself around, just in time to see the junkball fall into my glove.

The other St. James players are dying laughing as Ned

slinks back to the dugout. The next batter wastes his chance because he's so amused. He swings, giggling, at the first pitch and grounds out to short. Steve tosses it to David for the out. The batter doesn't even run it out but just shakes his head, snickering, and goes to the dugout.

"Come on, guys," says the coach. "I want to see quality at bats."

The third batter is the little brother of the minor leaguer. I know that the scouts are following this kid, too. He's supposed to be a big deal.

I signal for a fastball and put my glove low, and Sturgis delivers. The batter watches it go by.

"Ball," says the umpire.

So the hot prospect isn't going to swing away. I signal for a fastball at the belt, and Sturgis fires. The batter watches it go by again.

"Strike."

It's a good take, I know. He's timing Sturgis's pitches. He's seen two of them now. If we throw one more, he might nail it.

I signal for a seven, to change the batter's timing, and put my glove just on the inside of the plate. Sturgis delivers. The batter watches it go by.

"Ball." I myself think it had the corner, but there's no point arguing about it. I signal for the exact same pitch but move my glove a little back over the plate. The batter watches it go by.

"Strike."

I'm sweating. It's a good batter who can make you sweat

before he even swings the bat. I signal for a fastball and put my glove off the plate, just to see if he'll chase. He doesn't. He has good eyes, and he has patience. I also notice he's the only one not laughing at us. He's taking us seriously. I have to like the guy.

I also have to get him out, though. I signal for a changeup, flashing nine fingers. I wonder if Sturgis can slow it down just a smidgen.

He delivers, and the batter swings. There's a loud, hollow *thunk* as the aluminum bat nails the ball, and it sails deep into the outfield. Shannon catches it five or six feet shy of the warning track. It was a good piece of hitting, but he was a little bit in front of the pitch.

"Dumb luck," says the hitter on deck.

"It was a good pitch," the hot prospect tells him.

A 0 appears on the scoreboard below the 1. We've escaped the first inning without a base runner.

The fourth batter comes to the plate. He's the biggest guy on their team. I bet he plays football in the fall.

"I'll put an end to this nonsense," he says. He wags the bat eagerly, waiting for the fastball. He looks like he'll hit the ball into next week if we let him.

I have Sturgis throw nothing but fastballs. It's all about where I put my glove: I get the bruiser to swing over an inside pitch, then take one at the knees, then chase a pitch out of the zone. He swings his bat into the ground in annoyance.

"Better luck next time," I say casually, hoping he won't get another chance to bat.

The fifth batter lays a bunt toward third base. Miggy mishandles it, and the batter reaches first by a mile. I shout at Miggy not to even throw, worried he'll hurl the ball into right field.

Miggy is mad at himself and moves in a bit, daring the next batter to bunt. It leaves a big hole behind the base, but I'm not worried. Steve edges over, and he has good range. I am worried about Kazuo at second base, though. Does he know what to do if the ball comes to him? Does he know what to do if the ball goes to Steve? Most importantly, will he throw to the right base either way?

The sixth batter steps to the plate. He gives me a familiar nod, and I bet that he's the catcher. We tend to acknowledge one another as brothers-in-arms.

I signal for a fast pitch around the hands, and Sturgis delivers. The batter swings at it and bounces the ball toward Steve. I nearly close my eyes but force myself to watch: Steve fields the ball on the second hop and shovels it to second base without even looking.

Unbelievably, Kazuo is *there*, taking the ball, scraping the bag with his toe, turning a pivot that would make ballet dancers envious, and makes a perfect throw to David to complete the double play. It might as well be Tinker to Evers to Chance. It's so beautiful I want to cry.

A 0 appears on the scoreboard for the second inning.

We get into trouble in the third inning.

The seventh batter hits a lazy fly ball to left field. It

should be an easy out, but we have a ten-year-old in left field. It goes over his head and bounces off the wall. Shannon runs it down and gets it back to the infield, but the runner reaches third base.

Do we concede the run and settle for a tie or go for the win? I decide to play for the win and move the infield in to prevent a sacrifice bunt.

Sturgis strikes out the next batter, and we have a chance.

I want to set up the double play, so I signal for an outside pitch when the next batter comes up to bat. Sturgis glowers at me and shakes me off.

I call time and go out to the mound.

"Are you going to make me walk him?" he asks.

"We need to set up the double play," I explain. "Otherwise, a ground ball will score the runner from third."

"I hate this. I never want to put anyone on base."

"I understand that, but sometimes you have to play the percentages."

"It's their number nine hitter," he reminds me. "It's probably a pitcher."

"We don't know that. Since they don't have to play the field, they could have put anyone in that slot."

He sighs and consents to the intentional walk. The batter goes to first base.

Ned comes back to the plate with a smirk.

"This will be sweet," he says, taking a few practice swings.

I know it won't be easy the second time through the

lineup. They've seen Sturgis's stuff and will take better swings this time.

I signal for a fastball. Sturgis rears back and nails Ned in the stomach. Ned drops to the ground in pain.

"The kid's out of control!" he says when he catches his breath.

"That's it," says the coach playing umpire, making the sign umpires do for ejection. "This scrimmage is done."

"No way!" David yells. "You're just mad because we're winning."

"I'm not going to have my boys come up like ducks at a shooting gallery," the coach says.

"It was just an inside pitch," I lie. "The ball just got away from him."

"I know a beanball when I see one," says the coach. "You get off my field," he says, pointing at Sturgis. "The rest of you, too. We didn't sign up for this garbage."

"Aw, come on!" David is now running in from first to argue some more, but Peter waves him back and approaches the coaches to talk it over.

"I'll be right back," I tell them, and walk Sturgis out.

"You hit that guy pretty good," I say when we're out of earshot. "Knocked the wind out of him."

"Yeah," he says.

"I didn't like him either," I say with a shrug. "It wasn't a good time to throw at him, though. It loaded the bases with one out. Besides, they probably won't even let us finish now."

"I don't care," he says. "It was worth it."

"Hi," says Peter, exiting the ballpark. "I talked them coaches into letting you boys finish. They said I have to keep an eye on this one." He winks at Sturgis. "They're afraid he'll throw rocks through their windows if I don't."

Sturgis halfheartedly kicks a tire on the truck, not really looking at me or Peter.

I leave them both there and go back to the game.

"Sir, can we bring in another pitcher?" I ask the coach.

"Who is it?" he asks. "I don't want any more thugs throwing at my boys."

I point at Rita on the bench. He takes one look at her and rolls his eyes.

"Go ahead," he says with an exasperated sigh. "Bring her out." Under his breath, I hear something about a "freaking circus." Only he doesn't say "freaking" exactly.

Rita comes to the mound with the bases loaded. She looks scared. She prepares to warm up, but I signal at her to stop. I don't want anyone to see her screwball pitch.

"She doesn't need any warm-up pitches," I tell the umpire.

The next batter steps to the plate. It's the fellow who was laughing so hard in the first inning he grounded out on one pitch. He's laughing even harder this time. He takes a huge swing at Rita's first pitch. He might have knocked it to kingdom come if it was a regular pitch, but it's Rita's crazy screwball pitch. He grazes the ball with the top of his bat and bounces it back to Rita. The runners hold. Rita tosses the ball to David for the out.

As soon as she lets go of the ball, the runner on third takes off. David whips the ball back to me, and I'm able to get it and block the plate in plenty of time. The runner bowls into me, trying to knock the ball out of my hand, but I hang on.

The umpire signals the out. A third 0 appears on the scoreboard. We've won.

There's no handshakes, and nobody says "Good game" or "Thanks for coming." We just gather our things while the players begin their morning drills.

"Nice pitching," P.J. tells Rita.

She laughs. "I only threw one pitch."

"Two outs on one pitch. That's pretty good." P.J. is smooth, I have to admit.

"Well, we won," I say when we get out into the parking lot. "Good job, everyone."

"If it was a real game, they would have trounced us," says Steve.

"Maybe," I say. "We still did good."

"I wanted to hit," says David.

"Yeah, me too," says Miggy.

Peter's waiting alone in the cabin of the truck.

"Hey, what happened to Sturgis?" I wonder.

Peter just shrugs. "He said he had things to do."

Chapter 13

The return to Moundville is not exactly celebratory. The back of the truck is hot and dark and airless, and saps whatever energy we might have left. When we finally tumble out, everyone looks drained.

"Good game, Captain," Rita tells me quietly, casually touching my arm as she heads off for home. Shannon herself just nods and follows. The boys mumble that they'll see me tomorrow and scatter. We're acting like teams act when they've lost.

"I want to ride back to Sutton with you guys," I tell Peter when everyone is gone. "See what's going on with my brother."

"You don't have to do that," he says. "He said he'll walk to the home and garden store and catch a ride with your dad."

"I guess I will, too, then." I climb into the truck. P.J. slides into the middle, grumbling about losing the window seat.

"Sorry." I squish myself against the door, trying to take up less space.

"That was a pretty dumb move, what he did," Peter muses as he gets back on the highway. "Throwing at that boy."

"I know."

"I told him so, too. I thought St. James might offer him a scholarship, seeing what he can do. A school like

146

that? With their baseball team? It would have been good for him."

I gulp, thinking about Sturgis getting the red-carpet treatment at St. James when I can't even go anymore. Nobody ever thought about me getting a scholarship, but I guess I'm not special the way Sturgis is special. I'm good but not extraordinary.

I don't know if I'm mad at Sturgis for blowing it or a little bit relieved.

"What's he up to anyway?"

"He said he had stuff to do."

"So you don't know?"

"No," he says, but he's not a very good liar. I bet he knows exactly where Sturgis is or at least has a pretty good idea.

I think about Sutton. It's a big enough city that there are a dozen places a kid might go if he was bored and on his own. I guess most kids would head to either the mall or the business district near the river, where lots of hippies and skate punks like to hang out. Neither of those strike me as places that would tempt Sturgis, though. He hasn't shown much interest in shopping or being cool.

On the other side of town, there's not much in the way of fun stuff. Just houses and businesses. One business towers above all the others: the state prison.

"He's visiting his dad, isn't he?"

"I didn't even know his dad was at the penitentiary," he says innocently.

147

"I didn't say anything about the penitentiary. I just said he was visiting his dad."

"Oh yeah." Peter mutters at himself under his breath. I decide not to press, since he's driving us around and everything.

"Can we stop and eat?" P.J. asks as we hit the outskirts of Sutton.

"Do you want to?" Peter asks me. "I can treat." I'm glad he offers, because the second P.J. mentions food, I realize I'm really hungry, but I'm broke.

"I can pay you back later, but I didn't bring any money," I tell him.

"Don't worry about it." Peter pulls off at a divey little hot dog stand called Uncle Franky's.

We eat outside, dripping Uncle Franky's special sauce on our shirts. I'm usually a mustard and onion guy, but that sauce is amazing—kind of like mayo, but spicy. It complements the mustard and onion perfectly.

"So I was wondering about that Native American kid," I tell Peter between bites. "The one who didn't really drown."

"Ptan Teca?"

"Yeah, him. If he's, like, mad at us and everything, why isn't it raining anymore?"

"It's not about the rain," he says. "It never was about the rain."

P.J. gives me a look, and I guess that he's heard his father's theories far too many times.

"Well, what was it about, then?" I know I'm driving P.J. crazy by not dropping it, but I'm curious.

"Baseball," Peter says. "It was about baseball."

"Come on. I've never heard of an Indian curse being about baseball."

"You've heard of the curse on Moundville. They always lost to Sinister Bend."

"That wasn't a *curse* curse, though. It's just one of those things people make up because they can't explain why their team loses all the time."

"Ptan Teca loved baseball. He loved to beat the settlers at their own game. After he disappeared, the two teams kept playing, and his team won every time. I don't just mean for the next few years but every year for over a hundred years. You tell me that's just people making something up."

It could be explained by percentages. You take all the towns that play baseball against other towns, and one of those towns might put together a streak like that. At least, I think so. I don't know how to do the math. I don't think Peter would buy it, even if I did. I have a more practical question anyway.

"How could *his* team keep winning if the Dakota all had to leave?"

"By that time, there was no line to draw between white and Native American. The trading post had already been around for two or three generations. Everyone was a little bit of one or the other. If you were supposed to be a Native American, you had a German grandfather. If you were supposed to

149

be white, you had a Dakota grandmother. That's just how it was. Some of the Dakota left, but a lot of the people who stayed were a little bit Dakota in blood and spirit. The town that became Sinister Bend was made up of those people."

"So what was the curse? Sinister Bend beating Moundville every year?"

"I don't know if it was a curse exactly. A curse is when things go bad just because someone said they would. This was things going bad for Moundville because the spirits made them go wrong."

"Or maybe Sinister Bend was just better."

"You would think that if you never saw a game," he says. "You weren't there, though."

"I guess not."

"I saw nine games," he says. "Eight and a half, at least. Every year, you could feel the spirits at work. Swirling winds that carry balls into the gap. Rays of sunlight that would break through the clouds just in time to blind a fielder, allowing a ball to drop in. One year a crow squawked whenever Moundville batted and fell silent whenever Sinister Bend batted. If you were there, at those games, you knew that Moundville was meant to lose."

My dad tells some of those stories. He says they always felt doomed when they played Sinister Bend. I always thought it was just making excuses. Well, maybe Moundville was cursed or plagued by evil spirits or whatever. The only problem is, I don't believe in stuff like that.

"Why the rain, then?" I ask. "The rain didn't help Sinister

Bend win. The rain washed out a game they were a few outs away from winning."

At this point, P.J. gets up and just starts walking around, kind of agitated.

"You always assume things," Peter says.

"Like assuming Sinister Bend was going to win? They were ahead by *ten runs*."

"Moundville was getting to the pitcher, though. He'd thrown a bunch of pitches already, and they were catching up to him. I was batboy for that team, and I remember how worried we were about getting through the last couple of innings. We'd seen it happen before. When he lost the edge on his fastball, he could give up a dozen runs, easy. Once you figure out a pitcher, he's useless. Then that guy—your dad—he made our guy throw another thirty, forty pitches. We didn't have anyone else in our bullpen. I think it could have turned into a disaster."

"Are we going soon?" P.J. whines.

Peter ignores him. "Maybe Bobby Fitz would have come back, too. We never played by big-league rules where a guy can't come back after he leaves the game. Bobby just had a tweaked muscle. He still could have come back and sparked the team to a big rally. The rain prevented Moundville from turning it around."

"So you think the rain saved Sinister Bend?"

"That's a weird way to put it." Peter stands up and carries everyone's garbage to the bin. I think about the floods and realize he's right.

"Exactly! Why would the spirits drown the whole town?" I figure I have him there. "Maybe he'd wash out the game, but why would he wash out his whole hometown?"

"You don't know about Ptan Teca's temper. He's still just a little boy. The kind who holds his breath until he turns blue. The kind who takes his ball and goes home. The kind who tips a board game when he's losing and makes all the pieces fly around."

"Okay." It figures he'd have an answer for everything.

"Where do you want to go?" Peter asks me once we're back on the road. "The store where your dad works?"

"Might as well go straight to the prison," I tell him. P.J. groans, probably because the store is a lot closer than the prison. I look carefully along both sides of the street as we drive there, making sure we don't pass Sturgis on his way back downtown. We don't. Peter pulls into the parking lot of the prison and points off to the left of the truck.

"The store is a mile back that way. Walk straight there and don't take a ride if anyone offers. Call me if you need anything."

"Will do. Hey, you never did tell me why it isn't raining anymore. If that stuff about Ptan Teca is true, why did he stop it from raining all of a sudden?"

He ignores my question. "Seriously. Don't hitchhike or anything."

"No way. I'll call if I need a ride." I realize only after he's driven off that I don't even have his number.

There's a big door marked "Visitors," so I go on in and explain to a guard that I'm looking for Sturgis Nye, who's visiting Carey Nye. He looks at his registration book and nods.

"He's still there," he says. "You want to go in, too?"

"You mean I can? I'm not family or anything."

He shrugs. "This isn't the hospital. It's prison. You don't have to be family. Sometimes nuns just come by to visit anyone who wants company." He makes me sign a form and asks me to empty my pockets, but I don't have anything in them. We don't usually lock our doors in Moundville, so I don't even have a house key.

The guard buzzes the door, and I go into the visiting room. They don't have glass walls, like they do in the movies. It looks more like a school cafeteria, with the same kind of collapsible tables set up around the room and posters hanging up all over, with feel-good messages like "No Physical Contact of Any Kind" and "Clean Up Your Visitation Area or Disciplinary Action Will Be Taken."

Sturgis is not surprised to see me. "Hey, Roy," he says. "This is my dad."

"There he is," says Carey Nye, like he's expecting me. He has a shaved head now, but I recognize him from his baseball card and the photos I saw on the Internet. I offer to shake his hand. He holds up his own handcuffed hands, apologetically, and points to the sign about physical contact.

"I was telling him you might come," says Sturgis. "I told

153

him you were a big baseball fan and were excited to meet a real former major leaguer."

"I've read about you," I tell Carey. "You once pitched a no-hitter." I decide to focus on his best moment, never mind if it was in the minors.

"Yeah, I no-hit the Charlotte team. It wasn't easy," he says. "I think I threw about a hundred and fifty pitches. I thought my arm would fall off. I was crap for the rest of the season."

"It's still a pretty big achievement."

"Yeah," he says. "I guess so. You know who batted for the Knights in that game?"

"No, who?"

"Jim Thome."

"No kidding?"

"Struck him out twice," he says.

"Cool."

"He got me back," he says with a sigh. "When he was an Indian and I was an Oriole, he hit a grand salami off of me. Catcher made me throw a junkball." He shakes his head, remembering. "Whatever happened to Jim? Is he still with the Tribe?"

"He's with the White Sox now. By way of the Phillies."

"Hard to keep track of the standings in here, let alone players." He takes a deep breath. "Everyone thinks we have the Internet and cable TV, but it's not all that."

"Yeah," I say, as if I know from experience.

"So you're a catcher, huh? Catchers have it the worst,

man. It's torture. Your knees take a killing. You get run over at the plate and banged up by bad pitches. I don't know why anyone does it."

"They don't call the catcher's gear the tools of ignorance for nothing," I agree.

"You got that right," he says, laughing.

"Sturgis is quite a good pitcher, too," I tell him. "He's got a great fastball."

"Always knew this kid would be a good one," says Carey. "Remember the crab apple incident?" He laughs and slaps the table, rattling his cuffs.

"Oh yeah," says Sturgis. I can tell that for him, it's not such a treasured memory.

"I got called into his kindergarten because he was lobbing crab apples at kids on the playground," says Carey. "I mean, throwing them hard. He really nailed those kids. It looked like a scene from the *Godfather* movies, these four kids riddled with red splotches."

"I don't remember it very well," says Sturgis.

"I told the lady those kids just picked on the wrong guy," says Carey. "You were a mean little cuss, weren't you?"

"Yeah, I guess so."

"And then there was the rabbit. Oh, man. You're a chip off the old block, all right."

"Dad." Sturgis slumps back in embarrassment.

"My boy took down a jackrabbit at forty paces." Carey mimics the throw, rattling the cuffs. "How old were you, Sturgis?"

"I don't know."

"You were like eight or nine, since it was before I checked into this place. How many kids that age have done *that*?"

"Probably not many." Sturgis looks miserable.

"I was pretty proud of you," says Carey with a gleam in his eyes.

I get a weird déjà vu feeling when he says it. I can't quite figure it out, but it's something about Carey Nye. He doesn't look too much like Sturgis, but he looks familiar. Like somebody I've known for years.

"What made you think I'd come to the prison?" I ask Sturgis as we walk to the home and garden store.

"I couldn't see you doing anything else," he says.

"So why didn't you just ask me to come?"

"I don't know."

"I would have gone with you."

"You're that eager to meet a real big leaguer, huh?"

"Well," I start to explain, but I realize he's kidding me. He knows I'd go for him, not for me, and not for Carey.

"I think it was great what you did, making my dad feel like a big shot," he says. "Bringing up his no-hitter. That was cool. It meant a lot to him."

"Do you see him often?" I ask.

"Only a couple of times since he went in," he says. "You know, I saw him on the Fourth of July. That was the first time I even saw him since he went to jail. That was almost four years ago."

"So that's why you guys went to Sutton."

"Not so much for the fireworks, no."

"Did my dad go in, too?"

"Nah, he just dropped me off. Said he had friends of his own in Sutton he could visit."

"I guess he does." My dad has friends scattered around the state. "Why didn't you go before then?"

"My grandma. She didn't want anything to do with him after a while," he says. "She didn't want anything to do with the outside world anyway, but she especially didn't want anything to do with him."

"Oh yeah. You lived with your grandma."

"Yeah. This crummy old house in the middle of nowhere." He boots a stone and sends it skipping down the road.

"My dad said she couldn't take care of you anymore," I tell him.

"That's my fault," he says. "I went out to the highway and threw rocks at cars. I don't know why. Just to see if I could hit any, I guess. I did hit one, and it turned out to be an off-duty cop. I ran into the marsh, thinking he wouldn't follow me, but he did. One thing led to another, and they found out how I wasn't getting proper homeschooling or whatever. They decided Grandma wasn't fit to take care of me, and that's how I ended up with you guys. It's kind of bogus."

"It turned out all right," I say.

"I guess."

"Hey, do you still believe all that stuff about Ptan Teca and the curse?" I ask him.

"I don't know," he says. "Yeah, probably a little bit."

"Seriously?"

"Yeah. At least, I don't not believe it."

"Why do you think it stopped raining when it did?"

"It stopped just before the Fourth of July."

"So?"

"So I bet that Ptan Teca kid was hoping there'd be a baseball game. He finally got sick of waiting for the rematch."

"Hard to have a game with no teams and no field."

"Kids don't always think about stuff like that."

We've finally arrived at the store, just fifteen minutes before my dad gets off his Saturday shift. We go in through the lumber entrance and find him in his orange apron, telling a couple of other guys in orange aprons what to do. He does a double take when he sees us. He says something to the two workers and comes over to us.

"What are you guys doing here? For that matter, *how* did you get here?"

Chapter 14

On Sunday, my dad takes Sturgis to see his grandma, as usual. I camp out on the couch with Yogi, watching the Cubs play the Pirates. Mark Prior is having a good outing, and the Cubbies are winning. It's a pretty good game.

There's a knock on the door, and when I glance through the window, I forget all about the Cubs. It's Shannon and Rita, hanging out on my front porch. I gulp and go get the door.

"Um, what's up?"

They both look pretty cute. I'm used to seeing them a little scuffed up, wearing shorts and T-shirts. Now they're wearing the kinds of things the mannequins wear in the store windows of the mall in Sutton. I'm usually able to set my thing for Rita aside on the baseball field, but when she shows up at my house, kind of dolled up, I feel nervous and tongue-tied.

"We were wondering if you and Sturgis wanted to go get sodas or something," Shannon says. She's blushing a little.

"Sodas, huh?" I ask. "I feel like I'm in an Archie comic."

The girls laugh, and I loosen up a bit.

"Sturgis is out," I tell them. I explain how he sees his grandmother on Sundays. "I guess I could go, though, or we could wait for him to get back. You can come in, if you want."

They go about halfway down the walk to whisper to each other and decide what they want to do.

"We'll come in for a few minutes," says Rita finally.

"It's a nice house," says Shannon.

"Yeah," I say. "I've lived here my whole life. How long have you guys lived in Moundville?"

"We moved here about eighteen months ago," Rita says. "Cheap houses."

"About three years," says Shannon. "Same reason."

"So how do you guys know each other?"

"From Barrett," says Rita. Barrett is a private school in Sutton, the girls' equivalent to St. James. I think the two schools have box socials together or whatever private school kids do.

I notice Rita is carrying a book and ask her if I can see it. She holds it up, and I see it's *To Kill a Mockingbird*.

"I've read it like four times already," she tells me. "It's my favorite book."

"Yeah?" I've never read it, but I've seen the movie with my dad. "I think the black guy in that book is named Tom Robinson, same as Steve's dad," I tell her, which might be the dumbest thing anyone has ever said about a book.

"Oh," she says. "I guess it is."

The girls sit on the couch and make a fuss over Yogi until he gets tired of the attention and runs away.

"He's a pretty old cat," I explain. "He gets tuckered out fast."

"So," Shannon begins, but whatever she was going to

160

say gets lost on the way to her mouth. She looks to Rita for help.

"What happened to Sturgis anyway?" Rita asks. "We've been wondering."

"Nothing. He's just visiting his . . . ," I trail off, realizing what they really want to know. "You mean, what happened to his face?"

"I don't mean to be nosy."

"Oh, don't worry about it." I explain about the dogfight in Sutton.

"He had his ear ripped off by a dog?" Rita asks, looking at me with wide eyes.

"Yeah."

"I'm sorry. That story sounds a little made up."

"Well, that's what he told me." I remember how Sturgis told the story. Like it was something he'd seen in a movie. Or maybe read in a book, knowing him, although I bet in the book he stole it from it was a space alien instead of a wolf dog.

Shannon leans over to say something in Rita's ear. I turn my attention back to the ball game, the score of which doesn't register. I'm too preoccupied by the girls and Rita's suggestion that Sturgis lied to me. I guess it could be made up, but what if it was? Maybe the real story wasn't as good.

"So that's your favorite book, huh?" I ask Rita, trying to change the subject.

"Yeah. Do you have a favorite book?"

I am not, by habit, a big reader. I read part of The

Catcher in the Rye once but quit when it became clear that the guy telling the story wasn't going to play baseball, either as catcher or as anything else. I also read *The Natural* because that's my favorite movie, but in the book, the hero strikes out at the end. I felt cheated. So when she asks me my favorite book, the best one I can think of is *Catch You Later*, which is the autobiography of Johnny Bench.

"A baseball player wrote your favorite book," she says flatly after I tell her that.

I explain how Johnny Bench is probably the best catcher of all time, even better than Yogi Berra and Carlton Fisk, how he changed the image of catchers from dumb guys who didn't know better to smart guys who handle pitchers and manage the defense, and how he might have been more important to the great Reds teams of the seventies than even Pete Rose. So maybe I babble a bit. What can I say? I like Johnny Bench.

"I'm sure he's a great baseball player, but he's not really a writer. Do you read novels?" Rita asks.

"Sure," I tell her. "Sometimes."

"Suuure," she says, rolling her eyes. I think she's just kidding me, but I can see now what Steve said about her being a book snob.

"So do you think Sturgis will be back soon?" Shannon wonders.

"It's hard to say," I tell her. "Usually they're back around the seventh inning."

"You tell time by baseball games?"

"Well, I don't think to look at the clock when they walk in, is all." I realize I'm sounding dumber by the second and should quit while I'm ahead. "They could be back any minute."

They whisper to each other a bit.

"I think we should go," says Shannon.

"Oh?"

"We have to meet somebody."

"Well, I'll tell Sturgis you came by," I tell them. "And I'll try to read a novel. I promise."

"We'll see you at practice tomorrow." Rita smiles at me on her way out. Maybe she's just being nice, but I think it's kind of her way of saying, "It's okay. I like my boys dumb."

Sturgis and my dad get back about forty minutes later. I follow Sturgis into the bedroom so I can tell him about the girls dropping by.

"Yeah? They must have wanted to see you." He's changing out of his grandma clothes into jeans and a T-shirt.

"I don't know. I think they came to see both of us. They waited for you and everything."

"It's all for show." He's finished dressing and decides to forgo shoes. Instead, he grabs a book and sacks out on the bed. "I think Shannon digs you."

"I like Rita," I remind him.

"That's why Shannon wanted to blow. She saw you chatting up Rita and wanted to split."

"I don't know."

"Yeah, neither do I," he admits. I can see he's lost interest in the topic and wants to get back to his book.

"Hey, that reminds me, I need to read something." I look at his shelf of fantasy and sci-fi, a few odds and ends tucked in here and there—like that book about motorcycle maintenance.

"Do you have a favorite book?"

"I don't know. *Lord of the Rings*, I guess."

"You've read the whole thing? All three books?"

"Yeah," he says. "Like four times."

"I've only seen the movies."

"They made it into a movie?"

"Three movies. Wait—you never heard of the *Lord of the Rings* movies? They're only like the biggest movies ever."

"No, I just don't really see a lot of movies."

"Come on, everybody has seen the movies. Or at least *heard* of them."

"What do you want from me? My grandma never took me to movies, is all."

"Sorry. I'm just surprised."

"So is the movie any good?"

"There's *three* movies. They're pretty good."

"Probably not as good as the books," he says. "My dad gave me the whole set when he went to jail. I've read them probably five times. Every winter, I start over at the beginning. Man, I love those books. I've got the whole trilogy, if you want to read it."

"I don't know," I tell him. "It's pretty long, and I already know how it ends."

"Then don't. Your loss." He looks really disappointed in me. He just doesn't get that I'm not looking for a great reading experience. I'm just trying to make a good impression on a girl. None of Sturgis's books look like they would impress Rita—not if her favorite book is *To Kill a Mockingbird*.

I check my dad's bookshelf. He doesn't read much either, but he has a few books from when he was taking those night classes in Sutton. He doesn't have that book about the mockingbird, so I grab one called *Their Eyes Were Watching God*. The cover says it's a classic. I don't start reading it, though. I just set it on my dresser, thinking I'll read like a chapter a day.

Late that night, Sturgis suddenly wakes me up.

"Hey, Roy!" he whispers.

"Yeah, what?"

"How do they do Gollum? In the movie?"

"It's a computer animation."

"A cartoon? That sounds lame."

"It looks pretty realistic. They do amazing things with computers these days."

"I'd hate the movie if Gollum looked fake," he says. "He's my favorite character."

"Really?"

"Yeah. He was pretty cool."

"He's kind of a bad guy."

"I don't know," he says. "It's all in how you read it."

"Maybe."

"It's not all cut-and-dried," he says. "It's like being the visiting team in baseball. You're the bad guy, right? But when you're at home, you're the good guy. But you're the same guy, just doing your job, both times."

"Yeah, but Gollum kills people and stuff."

"The good guys kill people," he says. "Aragorn and Legolas and those guys."

"That's different. They just killed Orcs."

"So?"

"They aren't really people."

"Neither are Hobbits."

"It's different, and you know it."

"Sure, Roy," he says. He's quiet for a while.

"Anyway," he says, "I didn't say he was a good guy. I just said I liked him." He's snoring before I can think of a response. I'm just not cut out for literary conversations, I guess.

When I head to practice the next morning, I stuff my dad's book in my back pocket, like I'm so caught up in it I can't leave it behind.

When the players start scuffling in, a lot of them look a little down and aren't too eager to begin. The shabby treatment at the academy is still weighing on everyone. Anthony and P.J. don't even show up. It's pretty familiar from my Little League days. As you go along, some kids just stop coming.

"Hey, we're getting better," I tell the team before we start. It seems like a nice captainly thing to say. "We held those St. James guys scoreless for three innings."

"That's only 'cause we had Sturgis pitching," says Shannon. The others mutter their agreement.

"I remember outs recorded in the infield *and* in the outfield," I remind them.

"We didn't even get to hit," says David.

"Lucky for them!" I tell him. "Lucky for them."

He laughs a bit, and the others join in.

"I think we ought to play again," says Sturgis. "On our turf."

"Right," says Kazuo.

"We won't involve the grown-ups this time," he says. "It'll just be a sandlot game. Us versus them. No coaches. No umpires."

"They're not going to want to do that," says Steve.

"No. They won't want to. But they will," says Sturgis. "Unless they're chicken." He grins in his lopsided, slightly evil way, and I know what he's thinking.

"If you bait them, they will come," I say in my best *Field of Dreams* voice.

"I know exactly who I'm going to talk to, too," says Sturgis.

"That blond kid. The leadoff hitter," I say. "The smug one."

"Oh, I hated him!" says Rita. There's no doubt who we're talking about. I guess he got on their nerves, too.

"I think he'll be easier to poke than a dead possum," says

167

Sturgis. "Once he's poked, he'll get out here just to try and teach us a lesson."

"It might be learned the hard way," I say.

"It'll be worth it just to put another fastball in his rib cage," says Sturgis with a sly smile. I'm not at all sure he's kidding.

Sturgis's idea is a great motivator. Now the team is revved up, working hard on defense and batting balls all over the outfield in BP. They were never this stoked for the first game, but that was just about proving themselves. This is a lot more motivating: they want the other guys to *lose*.

After practice, I grab the book I've left sitting around in the dugout.

"Is that yours?" Rita asks me.

"Sure," I tell her. "I was thinking I should read a novel, you know. Something not by a baseball player."

"Roy, that book is about a middle-aged black woman who's been married three times."

"So?"

"So nothing," she says. "It's cute, is all. Let me know how you like it."

"So do you still want to do a soda?" I ask her, gesturing at the diner across the street.

"We're a little gross right now," she says with a laugh, which is true enough, I guess. We've had a hard practice, and it's a hot day. She pats my elbow as she leaves, and I can feel the cool of her hand long after she's gone, wishing I had been quicker with the maybe laters and how about tomorrows.

That evening, I go to the bedroom to read after an hour or so of television and a bit more dawdling on the computer. The book is depressing but pretty readable once you get used to the dialect. So much lousy stuff happens to her it makes for interesting reading.

No baseball, though. Not even Orcs.

Chapter 15

Sturgis has never used the Internet, so he asks me to find the blond kid from St. James. I'm able to find him with a little creative Googling.

I start with "St. James Academy baseball" and sort through the links until I find a recent box score. The box score only lists first initials and last names, but I guess that the leadoff hitter, N. White, is our boy Ned.

"Ned White" combined with "St. James Academy" doesn't get any hits on Google. By combining "N. White" with "St. James Academy," though, we get about sixty hits. One is a newspaper story that mentions Nicholas White as a college-bound basketball star from St. James who also lettered in track and baseball. So much for N. White.

"Do any of the players in the lineup have *E* for a first initial?" Sturgis is hovering behind me, trying to see the screen. "'Ned' is usually short for 'Edward.'"

"Are you sure?"

"I'm sure," he says.

"It should be short for 'Nedward.'" I Google the first of two names on the box score with the first initial *E*. A few seconds later, I'm on the MySpace profile for Edward Vandenberg.

"Ding-ding-ding!" It's totally the same guy. His profile picture is of him aboard a small boat, holding up a medium-sized fish. I figure it's the best he's got to show for himself—a good tan and a dead animal.

"Can you leave a note?" Sturgis asks.

"Sure," I tell him. I log in, navigate back to the page, and hit the button to leave a public message.

"Dear Needlenose," Sturgis dictates.

"Needlenose?"

"You got anything better?"

"Dear Ned," I type.

"It's too bad the boys' team wasn't there to play baseball the other day," Sturgis dictates. "We feel bad beating a bunch of girls, even though we have a couple of girls ourselves. Our pitcher tried to slow his pitches down so you could hit them, but he can only throw so slow.

"If you guys want to play a real game instead of that playground garbage we played last time, we'd be happy to see you on our home field. We'll bat and everything. I guess if you don't have anyone who can throw the ball all the way to the plate, you can bring a coach to pitch for you.

"Just let us know when you'll show up so we can warn the elderly and the faint of heart. We don't want them to die laughing.

"Yours truly, Roy McGuire." Sturgis finishes his dictation.

"Hey, I'm not putting my name on this thing."

"Why not? We're trying to get under his skin."

"If we want to show him we're not little kids, we can't act

like we are." I go back and edit the message, saying that we enjoyed the contest there in Sutton but were disappointed the coaches didn't let us play a full game. We'd be happy to host a game here, with no such fears of interference.

"Well?" Sturgis asks after I send the message.

"It's not like a phone call. He might not answer immediately."

"Drat."

It's barely five minutes before I see that I have a new message from the Nedinator, though. I click back to MySpace and see his reply.

"Fat chance!" it says.

"See where politeness gets you?" Sturgis asks. "Sign me up. Give me an account. I'll show you how it's done."

I set up an e-mail address for him on Yahoo, then a MySpace account. It takes longer than it should, since I have to explain e-mail to him and why you need an e-mail address to have a MySpace account.

"My grandma is trying to get me to use e-mail anyway," he says. "They have it at the home."

"It's pretty sad when your *grandma's* trying to get *you* to use the Internet," I tell him.

"If she knew e-mail was on the Internet, she'd probably be against it."

I finish setting up his account, telling the MySpace people he's fourteen so I can even do it.

"Go to," I tell him.

"Where do I find Needlenose?"

I reach over to show him how to access the browser history, but he's struggling with the mouse.

"Here." I take the mouse and do it myself.

"I can click this?" He takes the mouse back and clicks the Chat button. The Chat window pops up, and he starts typing furiously, using the two-finger hunt-and-peck method.

"Hit Return once in a while," I remind him.

It's hard to follow the chat over his shoulder, but he sure gets Ned to talk to him. He's pounding away, the Caps Lock on, using lots of exclamation points and accidental number 1s.

"Well, it looks like you know what you're doing," I tell him, and leave the room.

He catches me coming out of the bathroom a few minutes later.

"We're playing next week," he tells me. "Thursday at noon."

"All right."

"It's not against the proper St. James team, though. It's against Ned and some of his buddies."

"Even better."

"The only thing is . . ."

"Yeah?"

"I'm not completely sure if I signed us up for a baseball game or a rumble."

"We can always go over the ground rules before the game," I tell him. "To be on the safe side, I'll tell our team to bring both bats and gloves, and bicycle chains and switchblades."

"Oh, I can't wait to plug that kid," says Sturgis eagerly.

"Let's lay off the beanballs," I tell him. "It'll be way better just to beat them."

"Sure thing, Captain," he says. "If the game gets lopsided, though, I'm taking his head off." So much for the distinction between a baseball game and a rumble.

"So now can you show me how to e-mail my grandma?" he asks.

We have another week of practice, which is just long enough for motivation to flag but not enough time to get much better. My biggest worry is Sturgis's arm. Should I get his pitch count up, then rest him a couple of days? Let him pitch a little every day?

"Do you want to rest your arm at all?" I ask him.

"Nah. I'm fine."

"What's the most pitches you've thrown in a day?"

"I don't know. I used to practice throwing rocks just about all day. I never felt like I couldn't throw another one."

"Throwing rocks isn't as hard as pitching."

"You tell that to Peter Rabbit."

It takes me a second to figure out what he's talking about. "You won't just be plunking rodents this time."

"Not unless I have to," he says with a laugh. "Anyway, rabbits aren't rodents."

"What are they, then?"

"Rabbits."

"I'm glad we have that straightened out. Can you help Rita with her fastball? Just to humor me."

"Sure."

I'm a mite jealous watching the two of them, his massive hand wrapped around hers as he shows her the grip. So jealous I'm actually relieved when it's a disaster.

"She just can't throw straight," he tells me later. "Her trick pitch is a freak of nature."

"Oh well," I tell him. "I guess you should stop trying."

My other worry is the offense. P.J. is our best hitter, but he doesn't come every day, and he usually just wants to take batting practice. He's not much for fielding practice, which he needs a lot more.

"So are you on this team or not?" I finally ask him. "We'd love to have you, of course. We could use a good left-handed hitter in our lineup." For that matter, we need a good hitter in our lineup, but I don't tell him that.

"I've got a team," he reminds me.

"The Pirates? So why do you practice with us?"

"Something to do," he says with a shrug. "I come out here with my dad and get bored."

"Some of these guys think of you as a teammate."

"That's not my problem."

I guess I can't kick him off the team if he's not even on it. I wonder if I should flat out tell him not to come anymore. It's too bad we don't have a grown-up to make these decisions. A real coach would just tell a kid he's cut and that would be that.

I take it to the team. I dread their responses. I imagine David calling me out, telling me I'm just jealous because he's a better player than I am. I imagine Sturgis glaring at me, not saying a word but making me guess what he's thinking. Most of all, I imagine Rita standing up and stamping her foot, saying that if he goes, she goes, and leaving in a huff.

There's no way around it, though. I gather the team after practice.

I try to ease into the topic slowly.

"So that Peter kid, P.J. He's not too reliable."

"Nah," says David. "When he does show up, he hogs the plate."

"He bugs me," says Anthony.

"He's a good hitter, but he has his own team," says Sturgis. "He should just play with them."

"I agree," says Steve. "If he can't be bothered to show up, forget him."

"Let's tell him to get lost," says Rita. Rita says that!

"Wow, why didn't any of you say this stuff before?"

"We figured you wanted him on the team," says Steve. "You kept talking about what a great hitter he is."

"We thought you had a crush on him," says Rita with a grin. Shannon whacks her in the shoulder.

"Well, I guess that's that, then." I'm thinking that was pretty easy—then I remember I still have to tell P.J. the bad

176

news. I never get the chance, though, because he never comes back to a Moundville practice.

When Sturgis gets back from his visit to Grandma on Sunday, he wants to pitch a bit.

"Did she get your e-mail?" I ask him as we head out back.

"Yeah. I told her about us being on MySpace, and she got worked up about it. She's been seeing stuff on the news."

"Just don't talk to any weirdos and you'll be fine."

"Too late. I talked to Needlenose, remember?"

"Right."

We start to toss the ball back and forth, not really working on anything, just throwing the old beanbag around. Sturgis has naturally good mechanics. Even casual pitches are fluid, straight, and on target. Also hard. The guy has a cannon for an arm.

"Your grandma going to come to the game?" I ask him.

"Huh?"

"She could come and watch."

"I didn't realize there would be spectators."

"It's not like no one will see us. The game is downtown, in broad daylight. It'll probably draw a crowd. At least a little one."

"Yeah, I guess so," he says. "How do you think the other guys will take it?"

"Well, they have to get used to it sooner or later."

"There's no bleachers," he reminds me. It's true, but for some reason I hadn't thought of it. The old, ruined bleachers were finally dragged off to the dump, but there's no new ones yet.

"People will watch anyway," I tell him.

"We're going to need bleachers eventually," I tell my dad after supper. "If there's ever a game, you know. People might want to watch." For the time being, I'm not letting on about our game against Ned's posse, but I figure we ought to start thinking about the future.

"Oh, right," he says. "I'm working on it." He seems agitated, though, and I figure he's run out of money and connections for renovating the ballpark. He's also working at the store a lot, so it's hard for him to even make calls and cut deals anymore.

"No hurry," I tell him.

"No, no. You're right. There's no point in having a baseball field if there's no way to watch a game. Let me make some calls."

I've given up on Rita, or at least I've pretended to. Even with P.J. out of the picture, she seems pretty indifferent to sodas or anything else that would improve upon our captain-player relationship. I tell myself I'll move on, but I find myself thinking about her off and on all the time.

One day during practice, she asks me if I'm enjoying Zora Neale Hurston.

"Who?"

"She wrote the book you're reading? *Their Eyes Were Watching God?*"

"Oh, right." I'm glad she wants to make small talk, but I haven't picked it up in a while. "I haven't had much time to read it lately."

"Riiiiight," she says. I don't really know if she's kidding anymore or sort of put out with me because I'm illiterate.

"What about you?" I ask in a friendly way. "What are you reading these days?" She tells me about somebody's memoir until my eyes glaze over.

"It's good," she says at last.

"It sounds interesting," I lie.

"Well, see you around," she says. I feel like I've failed a test and vow to read ten pages in that book about the woman with all the bad marriages before I go to bed.

Word gets around about the game. It's not exactly like the games of yore, but a few dozen people show up with lawn chairs and coolers on the day of the game, settled down for an afternoon of baseball. It is during the workday, so there's not a lot of parents. Dad is working at the store, for example.

At least all the players show up.

"You guys nervous?" I ask the team. "We have spectators this time."

"Nah," says David.

"We've played tennis in front of people," Shannon says, meaning her and Rita.

"We've played basketball in front of people," says Miggy, meaning him and Tim.

"I was in a school play," says Carlos.

"I'll be okay," says Kazuo.

An SUV pulls alongside the park, and as soon as the team spills out, we know we're sunk. The kids are fresh out of T-ball. I'd be surprised if any of them has seen his ninth birthday.

"What the heck is this?" asks David.

"The old switcheroo," says Steve.

"I *hate* that 'roo," says Rita.

"Roy? Roy McGuire?" Needlenose is playing coach, wearing khaki shorts and a polo shirt, with a whistle slung around his neck and expensive sunglasses tucked into his collar. I'm surprised he's old enough to drive. He didn't look *that* much older than us.

"We should have seen this one coming," says Sturgis, his annoyance tinged with respect.

"Let's get out there," I tell him. "I think we can make a game of it."

"Yeah, right. Pitching to toddlers. My favorite sport."

I walk out to meet Ned near the plate, my teammates skulking behind me, a dozen feet back.

"Come on, guys," I tell them. "Let's introduce ourselves." We shake hands with the gaggle of young boys Ned has brought.

"You're old," says one of the boys matter-of-factly.

"Don't worry," says Ned. "You guys are a lot more experienced, so it evens out."

"Well, let's pick teams," I announce.

"Um, that's not how it's done." Ned looks at me around his nose. It isn't fair to say it's a needle. It's long, sure, but not nearly pointy enough to use as a sewing instrument. It looks more like a fungo bat. "Your team is supposed to play our team."

"Let's just pick teams instead," says one of his players, and his teammates rapidly agree. Ned looks a little blue in the face but doesn't put up much of a fight.

"But I've got plans!" he says. "We have to be back in Sutton by three o'clock."

"Well, you knew there would be a game this afternoon," Rita reminds him.

He sighs, pulls out a cell phone, and wanders off.

"Who's your pitcher?" I ask the boys.

One of the boys timidly raises his hand. He has the same whitish blond hair as Ned, and I suspect he's a little brother.

"Okay, why don't you be a captain? And, Rita, you too. That way both teams have a pitcher. You pick first." I clap my hand on the boy's shoulder.

"Are you playing?" he asks me.

"Oh yeah."

"Then I pick you!"

"I need a catcher," says Rita. "Who's a catcher?" A pudgy boy raises his hand, and she picks him.

After that, it's easy enough to divide up into equal teams. We more or less go by positions through the right fielders. There's more of them than us, though, so I just assign the last few kids to teams rather than force one of them to be the last one picked.

I'm on a team with David, Miggy, Shannon, and five or six kids, including Carlos. The other team is Rita, Kazuo, Steve, Anthony, Tim, and the rest of the kids.

"We're the Orcs," I tell the kids.

"We'll be the Hobbits, then!"

Since they picked first, we get to be the home team. As my team of Orcs takes the field, I realize that Sturgis isn't even among us anymore. He's disappeared.

I walk casually over to the small crowd of onlookers.

"Anyone want to be umpire?" I ask.

Chapter 16

Sturgis is stretched out on the couch, petting Yogi and reading a book called *Stormbringer*. Based on the title, it's probably the last book anyone else in Moundville would want to read.

"How was the game?" he asks.

"Pretty good. The Orcs won." It was actually a great afternoon, I tell him. Nobody took the game too seriously, but we played for seven and a half innings. The Orcs officially won in the bottom of the seventh, taking a six-to-five lead on a badly fielded grounder that scored a run. We didn't want to win that way, though, so we gave them an extra half inning to bat. The crowd stuck around for every pitch.

"We missed you," I tell him at last.

"I can't pitch to little kids," he says. "It wouldn't be right."

"You could have played another position."

"You haven't seen me play other positions," he says. "It isn't pretty." I think it's sad that Sturgis is worried about how he looks among some little kids but decide not to pursue it.

"Ned was a no-show for most of it, too," I tell him. "He came back around the fifth inning and was so impatient I thought he'd explode." I was proud of those kids for playing on, ignoring his threats and pleading. Our pitcher silenced him at once by saying he'd "tell Mom" how Ned had taken the car out with just his learner's permit.

"You should have seen his face when I suggested the extra half inning," I tell Sturgis. "It was priceless. That was half the reason I suggested it."

"Not as good as a fastball to the sternum, but at least he learned a lesson," he replies.

I'm not being completely level with Sturgis. The mixed-up game with the Little Leaguers from Sutton was fun, but it wasn't satisfying. We were out for blood and got Kool-Aid.

It's not just wanting to beat St. James, though, or even beating Needlenose Van Fungobat at his own game. We've played a couple of exhibitions now, but we still haven't gone toe to toe with a real opponent. As I walk into the bedroom, I glance at my baseball from Adam and get a great idea: our gang of newbies could play his team of all-stars.

My mom calls on Friday. She hasn't called for a couple of weeks, but it feels like a lot longer. She's calling from Lisbon, Portugal, this time. She was an attendant on a flight out there and is allowed to take a day to herself before she works on a flight back. It's early in the evening here but must be past midnight there. She sounds like she's been having a good time. It's slurry, incoherent Mom, not creepy, knows-everything Mom.

"There's no baseball on the Iberian Peninsula," she says, stumbling on the word "Iberian" and rhyming "Peninsula" with "Venezuela." I can send you a postcard of a soccer stadium, though."

"That would be okay."

184

"Do you have any idea how crazy they are about soccer here?"

"I've heard they're pretty crazy about soccer everywhere."

"There was some kind of big tournament here. Well, not here exactly, but I guess there was some kind of big tournament. And Portugal did really well. Everyone's talking about it."

"I'll bet."

"Is it the World Series of Soccer?"

"Mom, it's called the World Cup."

"Right. Anyway, the Portugals did really well. I think they won or something."

"They got fourth place." Miggy and Anthony were following the World Cup pretty closely and talked about it a lot.

"Really? Because people here are acting like it's a big deal."

"Fourth place is really good for the World Cup," I tell her. "There's lots of countries, you know."

"That is so true! People say that it's a small world, but you know, it's not small. It's really big," she says. "It's really, really big."

"Yeah," I agree, afraid she'll start singing "It's a Big World After All."

"So is it still not raining in Moundville?"

"Not all the time anymore, no. I've got a baseball team and everything." I tell her a little bit about the team.

"That's wunnerful," she says. "I'll have to come see you play. I don't think I've ever seen Moundville win a game!"

She laughs. "I only ever really saw the games against Sinister Bend. Do you think they'll play a rematch?"

"There's no Sinister Bend, really," I remind her.

"They'd probably play you." Sometimes she's not a very good listener. "Why wouldn't they? It's a tradition. Plus, they always win."

"There *is no* Sinister Bend." I try to speak louder, just in case it's a bad connection.

"Well, it's late here. Goodbye." She clicks off, forgetting to say she loves me and not letting me tell her.

Through extensive e-mails and IM sessions, Adam and I are able to schedule a game on the university campus where we went to baseball camp. The town is nearly halfway between Moundville and Adam's hometown.

Half of us pile into Mr. Robinson's SUV, the other half into one driven by Kazuo's mom. She turns out to be the more fearless driver and leaves us in the dust while Mr. Robinson drives the speed limit.

"Most people go five or ten miles over the limit," Steve says as the other car disappears in the distance.

"What's the hurry?" Mr. Robinson asks, tapping the digital clock. "We're making excellent time. Anyway, I've got a special musical program just for the occasion." He takes out a CD marked "Part 1 of 4," and I know we're in trouble.

The university has everything a college is supposed to: stately buildings covered with ivy, spacious lawns with trees perfectly placed for sitting under while reading a book, and a football stadium that rises above it all like a cathedral. Behind that stadium are practice fields, tennis courts, and a narrow river in which preppies probably shout "Bully!" and "Port ho!" to dapper crews in vests and white caps. It's all very collegiate.

There are also four baseball diamonds, which all come in handy when softball and baseball camps are under way but are relatively unused otherwise. So says Adam's older brother, who even signs one out to his fraternity's nonexistent softball team to be sure.

We get started around 2:00, a bit later than we planned, but still with enough time to play and get home at a decent hour.

It turns out to be a short game anyway. Adam has stuff even I haven't seen, making the ball twist around our bats like it's a Wiffle ball. Sturgis has his fastball working but changes speed enough that the other guys are always guessing when to swing and never guessing right. Both pitchers are in the groove, and the innings fly by.

After six regulation innings, it's not even 4:00. Nobody's had a runner on third. We're all hot and tired, though, and I just want someone to win so we can go home—so long as the someone is us.

"How's your arm?" I ask Sturgis.

"Like I said," he tells me, "I can pitch all day. My arm never gets tired."

Adam is not so lucky. In the top of the seventh, with one out, he drops enough balls in the dirt to walk Steve, then waves off his coach so he can keep pitching. I know that kids can get injured throwing too many pitches, especially curveballs. I want to run out to the mound and tell him there's a lot more riding on this game than a win, but I also know Adam well enough to know how pointless it is. He's like the knight in the movie who loses an arm and calls it a flesh wound.

He hangs a curveball on Tim, who bloops it past their shortstop. Steve runs all the way to third base. Adam curses audibly and looks like he might cry.

Sturgis is the next scheduled batter.

"I'm pinch-hitting for you," I tell him. "Anthony, you're up!"

"Does that mean I can't pitch next inning?" Sturgis asks.

"I don't know." Unlike pro ball, Little League rules are pretty flexible about taking players out of the game and putting them back in again. I'm worried about Sturgis, though. Even if he says he can throw all day and not get hurt, the truth is that a kid can wreck his arm forever if he strains himself.

"Right now I want someone who can get a base hit. We'll decide who pitches when it's our turn to pitch."

"I'm fine. I can pitch as long as you need me to." He hands the bat to Anthony and goes back to the dugout.

"Bring 'em home, Tony!" I holler.

He does, flying out to left field, deep enough that Steve can score. We're all hugs and high fives at the plate, except

Sturgis. Rita herself gives Anthony such a hug I'm a mite jealous, although it's nothing compared to the way he squeezes Shannon.

I slide over by Sturgis on the bench. "I'm going to have Rita close the game. Show them something different."

He just grumbles at me.

"Fine. Be that way."

Adam's team is relieved to see Rita take the mound in the bottom of the seventh, since they've had no success against Sturgis. That is, until they find themselves flailing helplessly at her screwball. They get a base runner but strand him on second.

"See, we won," I tell Sturgis. "Come on, let's go shake hands with those guys."

He just looks at me with mean, hurt eyes and refuses to budge.

I'm thrilled when Rita clambers aboard Mr. Robinson's SUV after the game. She sits next to me, which may or may not mean anything.

"Switching horses, eh?" Mr. Robinson asks her.

"I needed to make room for Sturgis. He wanted to ride back with them."

Ride back without me is more like it, I think.

"It's all right with me, though." Rita shudders visibly. "The way that woman drives scares me."

"I'm a big fan of traffic safety," I tell her. "My aunt Evelyn died in a car accident."

189

"Oh!" She looks at me sadly.

"It's okay," I say. "I didn't really know her." As usual, when I'm talking to Rita, everything I say is dumb.

"Well, you're in luck," Mr. Robinson announces. "I've got some great music lined up for the trip home. Sam Cooke. Otis Redding. Etta James."

"Sounds great," says Rita politely. I realize for the first time that her hair smells like raspberries and she has a few small pimples covered with a brownish cream. I knew they made pink pimple cream that didn't look at all believable on white skin, but I didn't know they also made pimple cream that didn't look at all believable on brown skin. In a weird way, it's interesting. Both the raspberry smell and the cream make me like her more.

She edges away from me, and I realize that studying a girl's blemishes in fascination isn't a very good way to woo her. I'm unable to recover with anything clever, so we ride back in silence, barely mumbling to each other when the car hits a bump and sends one of us crashing into the other.

In the back, Steve and Tim are whispering to one another. I can't really hear them but catch occasional words and phrases.

". . . not much of a team player," Steve is saying.

"Always been a jerk to me," says Tim.

They're obviously talking about Sturgis. I don't have the energy to defend him, though. Besides, what could I say?

That he didn't brood and pout after the game? That he was full to the brim with team spirit?

Maybe I'll talk to him later, I decide. Probably not tonight but maybe tomorrow.

Eventually, I slide down into my seat, resting my knees on the back of the seat in front of me. My knees are pretty sore after the game, and a long, cramped drive is the last thing I need. I close my eyes and doze off to the soothing voice of Sam Cooke over the car stereo and the intoxicating smell of raspberries.

Thanks to Mrs. Obake's NASCAR approach to highway driving, Sturgis is home long before me. When I come in, he's helping my dad make supper.

They bustle about in the kitchen, muttering in low voices, while I rub my aching knees with ointment and stretch out on the couch. I think they're talking about gazebos and patios and whatnot. Sturgis takes a lot more interest in my dad's work than I do. Yogi hops up on the couch and tries to lick the menthol ointment off of me, which is one of his more disgusting habits.

I finish reading *Their Eyes Were Watching God*, which ends with the woman's third and favorite husband getting bitten by a rabid dog and her living in disgrace because she has to kill him when he was all rabid and crazy. It makes me wonder why great literature always has to end horribly. Can't anyone live happily ever after?

Also, the stuff with the dog makes me think about Sturgis and his dog bites, and Peter's mumbo jumbo about spirit animals and all that. I've never been bitten by anything interesting. Not even a radioactive spider.

Dinner is stuffed squash. The squash isn't stuffed with anything that weird—just ground beef, onions, and a bunch of spices. It's one of my dad's better meals. I'd think maybe Sturgis was giving him some advice, except that Sturgis will eat anything.

"So are you going to tell me about the game?" Dad asks.

I'm too tired to talk but halfheartedly describe the game. I compliment Adam's pitching but say that in the end he was no match for Sturgis.

"I didn't pitch in the end," Sturgis reminds me, still brooding about getting pulled in the last inning.

"Huh?" my dad asks.

"I pinch-hit for Sturgis and let Rita close the game."

"Who's this Rita? You have a girl on the team?"

"A couple," I tell him.

"Well, what do you know?"

It stuns me to realize my dad has never seen all of us play, not even for a full practice. He's really supportive at home, but he's been busy with his new job, plus trying to get his business off the ground. My dad's a workaholic. Even when there's no real work to do, he just creates busywork for himself.

"I got stuff to do," says Sturgis when he's done eating. He shoves his plate aside and goes off to the office, maybe to e-mail his grandma.

"He's a bit of an odd duck," my dad says in a low voice, "but he's a good kid, don't you think? They told me he might be trouble, but I haven't seen it."

"He is," I tell him, but the way it comes out, it's not clear which statement I'm agreeing with.

Chapter 17

"You all right?" I ask Sturgis when we're getting ready for bed.

"Why wouldn't I be?"

"You were sort of upset about the game."

"It's only a game," he says with a shrug. "So maybe you made a mistake as manager, but all's well that ends well."

It's hard to argue that I made a mistake when all ended well, but I let the remark slide.

"I pitched pretty good, right?"

"You were fantastic."

"I could have pitched ten more innings," he says. "I could go pitch again tomorrow. My arm feels great."

"That's good news."

"Do you think I'm ready?"

"Ready for what? You already pitched against a good team and won. I think you're there."

"All right, then." He seems satisfied, and I edge in with my agenda.

"So maybe next time we play, you can act like a member of the team? You know, the handshakes and all that. It's part of the game."

"I was never much for the formalities."

"The other guys—" I start to say.

"What?" His voice takes on an edge. "The other guys what?"

"I was just going to say that the other guys were asking if you were okay."

"You can tell them I'm fine."

"Well, next time, maybe go along with the formalities. Just so they don't worry about you."

"Sure," he says. "It's no big deal." To prove it, he's sound asleep a few seconds later.

"So do you want to come with?" Sturgis asks me in the morning. He's groomed and ready to go by the time I wake up.

"Huh?"

"Come see my grandma."

"Really?"

"Why not? You met my dad. She can't be any worse than him, right?"

"She's just in a nursing home, at least," I tell him. "Not in prison."

"Exactly."

"I guess." Visiting old people isn't high on my list of fun things to do, but I figure it's a good start at mending the little feud we had yesterday. Also, I'm a bit curious. So I take a quick shower and put on my cleanest jeans and a kind of Hawaiian shirt that looks nice and not too gaudy. Just festive.

"Lookin' sharp," says my dad when he sees me. "Got a date? Maybe with this Rita?"

"No," I tell him, feeling myself redden. It's a lucky guess on my dad's part that I'm even interested in Rita. "I'm going with you guys."

"No kidding. Did Sturgis say you could come?"

"He asked me to," I explain.

Sturgis's grandmother lives in Temple Village, a retirement community a few miles short of Sutton down the highway. It's a gray little cluster of buildings poking above the yellow prairie. There's a stiff wind blowing, which is probably why the terrace and grounds are empty, even with the sun shining.

My dad has brought the Sunday paper and now settles into a comfy-looking chair in the lobby to read while Sturgis leads me up a flight of stairs and down a long hallway that smells like asparagus.

"Don't mention baseball," Sturgis suddenly whispers as we approach the end of the hall.

"Huh?"

"She doesn't know I play," he explains. "She wouldn't like it."

He knocks loudly, and we hear coughing and scratching about until the door finally opens.

She's not even that old, I think. No older than Steve's grandma, who's still working and always doing things, and nowhere near the retirement home kind of lifestyle.

Sturgis's grandma is a little worse for the wear, though. There's a yellow tinge to her skin and eyes, and she smells funny. There's something weary and broken about her. She's sick with something, I know. It must be one of those long, drawn-out diseases that destroy you in slow motion.

"Oh, it's you," she says. "You've brought a friend?"

"This is Roy," he tells her. "Remember, I told you about Roy?"

"Of course I remember Roy," she tells him crossly. "My liver isn't working right, but my brain is." She nods hello to me but doesn't notice the hand I offer.

"Come in, come in," she says. "I'm making soup."

The kitchen is just a little open area off to the side, not a proper room. I can see potato peels and carrot shavings in the sink and something bubbling on the stove. I'm a bit scared of eating anything made in this place, but it smells okay. Just vegetables, I tell myself. Vegetables probably can't hurt you.

"It won't be ready for a while," she says to me. "You hungry now?"

"No, ma'am," I tell her.

"'Ma'am,'" she repeats with a weak smile as she walks slowly back to the living room to sit down. "He's a polite one, Stuey."

"I told you, he's a nice guy." Sturgis sits by her on the couch, and I take a dining room chair, since there's pretty much nowhere else to sit.

"Well, I'm glad you have a friend," she says, plopping down on the couch. "Sturgis never had friends," she explains.

"Grandma," he says in disbelief.

"Well, it's true," she says. "It's my fault, I guess. I should have moved to Moundville instead of living in the old farmhouse out in the middle of nowhere."

"So your family is originally from Moundville?" I ask.

"Oh, we're not from Moundville," she says. "Them's fighting words," she adds with a wheezing laugh.

"Sinister Bend," Sturgis explains.

"You never told me that."

"Didn't I?" He won't look at me for some reason. "Well, I never lived there myself. Just Baltimore and out at the farmhouse."

"Right." I try to incorporate Sinister Bend into the Nye family history.

"It was probably a mistake to homeschool, too." His grandma is still obsessing over her mistakes. "But what else could I do after you got kicked out?"

"Crab apples?" I whisper to Sturgis.

"Different occasion," he whispers back. "Hey, do you want to watch a movie or something?" He picks up the remote.

"We're talking, Sturgis." She reaches for the remote, and he hands it to her. She puts it down in front of her.

"I suppose you know about Sturgis's dad?" she asks me.

"Mostly," I tell her. "I know he's in prison."

"It's true. My boy's a jailbird," she says with a sigh. "You try to keep your boys out of trouble, but they always find it. He fell in with the wrong crowd, he did. That and the devil music and the trashy novels, he never had a chance."

Sturgis rolls his eyes. He's inherited all of his father's books and music, after all.

"I tried to keep this one out of trouble," she says of

Sturgis. "He was getting into fights at school, so I took him out." She's just said he was expelled, and now she's trying to cover her tracks. "Who knows what goes on in schools anymore anyway?"

"He turned out okay," I tell her, wondering how Sturgis kept his hard-rock tapes and Orc books hidden from her when he lived there.

"I don't know what inspired him to throw rocks at cars," she says. "You can't pin that one on me."

"Kids just do dumb things," says Sturgis. He's looking longingly at the TV, and I guess he usually tries to pass the time by finding a movie rather than talk about the past for two hours.

"You might think he did it just to get me in trouble," she says thoughtfully.

"That's stupid," says Sturgis quietly.

"Maybe I didn't do enough!" she suddenly says, as if the thought has just occurred to her. "Was I a bad grandma?"

"Grandma, you say the same thing every week. Nobody said you were a bad grandma, just that you were sick."

"I don't know about that," she grumbles. "You were at the hearing. You heard what they said." She punctuates her despair with a short fit of coughing.

"You did a good job with Sturgis," I tell her. "He's not going to turn out like his dad."

She looks at me for a long time, her lower lip trembling, and I'm not sure if she's going to cry and thank me, or yell at me to mind my own business.

"Well, I'm glad you have friends," she says, but she's not looking at Sturgis, she's looking at me. It's weird. It's almost like she's accusing me of something. Maybe she's assuming my friends are also the wrong crowd and we'll lead Sturgis astray.

"Let's play Scrabble," says Sturgis.

"How was it?" my dad asks when we finally make our way downstairs after a bowl of flavorless vegetable soup and three games of Scrabble, two won by Grandma and one won in a squeaker by Sturgis. Grandma didn't have a dictionary handy, and I think she made up words. I'm pretty sure Sturgis made up "jonquil" to win the last game and intend to google it as soon as we get home.

"Sorry for such a boring afternoon," Sturgis says on the drive home. We're both riding in the back, so we can talk. "I figured it would be less torture if you were there."

"It wasn't that bad," I tell him. It really wasn't.

"My grandma. She hasn't really forgiven herself."

"What, for not taking care of you?"

"Nah. She tried. I mean my dad. She hasn't forgiven herself for my dad. You know, turning out the way he did."

"That's too bad. It's not her fault he's such an—" Here I almost stop myself but don't. I use a word you probably can't use in Scrabble.

Sturgis glares at me.

"Oh, come on. I didn't mean it to come out like that."

"Sure you didn't."

200

"Well, he is one. Kind of. You have to admit."

"I don't talk trash about your dad."

"Guys?" My dad hears us arguing but doesn't know what we're talking about. "Is everything all right?"

"We're fine," says Sturgis, sinking into the corner and glowering. Nice way to treat a guy after he goes to see your dad in prison *and* your grandma at the home, I think. Not to mention sharing his bedroom and teaching you an off-speed pitch.

I do a little sinking and glowering in my own corner.

As soon as my dad pulls into the driveway, Sturgis is climbing out of the truck. It's awkward because it's a two-door and you're supposed to spring the seat forward, but Sturgis crawls over it. He looks a little bit like Gollum, in the movie.

"Is everything all right?" my dad wonders.

"I'm going for a walk," Sturgis says as he finally gets out of the truck.

My dad nods and looks like he's thinking of something fatherly to say. "Be home by dark," maybe, or "Stay out of trouble." Before he can come up with anything, Sturgis is nothing but a long-legged dot in the distance and fading fast.

My dad and I watch a West Coast game on ESPN that evening and fill up on pizza and popcorn. The Yankees are playing the Angels. Both teams score a bunch of runs.

Around the seventh inning, we're startled by a boom of thunder. I glance out the window. Dark clouds are moving in. The thunder booms again, there is a flash of lightning, and rain begins to pour down.

"It's just a regular old rain," says my dad.

"I know," I say. "I'm glad. The baseball field needs it."

We sit through the end of the game. The rain continues, and Sturgis still doesn't come home.

"He must be waiting out the storm somewhere," says my father. He looks upset, though. "Do you think I should call the police?" he asks a bit later. "Would that be overreacting?"

"I don't know," I tell him. "He's probably okay. He's taken care of himself a lot."

"This is true," says my dad.

"He might want a ride, though," I say. "We should go out looking for him."

"All right," my dad says. We turn off the television and grab our ponchos.

We drive around, listening to the radio, which gives us nonstop advice to get back inside. We stop downtown, and I check the shadows of both dugouts while my dad pokes his head into the pool hall and the bar, just in case Sturgis is getting into trouble after all.

"I don't think he'd go back to his grandmother's," my dad says.

"No, me neither."

"Is he good friends with anyone on the team?" my dad asks.

"Not especially."

We drive aimlessly, past darkened stores and rows of

houses. My dad turns around in the circular driveway of the school.

"I think we should head home," he says uneasily. "We can't drive around all night."

"Nope," I agree.

We take a long route, hoping to catch a glimpse of a wet boy hurrying along on the sidewalk.

"He might even be home when we get there," I tell my dad.

He isn't, though, and there are no messages.

"He must be waiting out the storm," says my dad again. "I'll call the police in the morning if he doesn't call."

We watch some old comedy reruns on TV and wait. I drop off to sleep and have crazy dreams. When I wake up, it's stopped raining, and my father is asleep in the chair. The television is off.

Sturgis is slumped in the other chair, drowsy but awake.

"What's up?" I ask.

"I guess you are."

My dad opens his eyes and looks around in confusion before he remembers where he is.

"Must have nodded off," he says. "What are you boys doing up? And you," he says, pointing at Sturgis. "You have to let me know where you're going from now on. And you ask permission, and you don't stay out late. I'm not running a youth hostel."

"I was just with P.J.," says Sturgis.

"Who?" My dad looks puzzled.

"Peter Labatte's son," Sturgis reminds him. "I ran into him, and we went over to help his dad with this place he was working on, and then the storm came and we holed up there. There's no phone there. He has a cell, but with the storm . . ." He shrugs. "As soon as the storm let up, he dropped me off."

"All right, then," my dad says, too tired to stay angry. He's not so good at the traditional dad stuff, like yelling or laying down the law. He doesn't tell Sturgis how we drove around in the storm trying to find him.

"We talked a lot about baseball," Sturgis tells me. "Peter says he's ready for the rematch."

"Huh? Which game?"

"Moundville versus Sinister Bend. What else?"

"There is no Sinister Bend team."

"That's what you think."

Chapter 18

Even though none of us have had proper sleep, the three of us have to go to Sutton in the morning. Sturgis and I need to register for junior high.

Sturgis's records are complicated, what with the "home-schooling," so the school wants him to take tests to figure out how to place him. He's the right age for seventh grade, though, so they tentatively let him register for the usual slate of classes.

Afterward, Sturgis and I walk out of town and down a muddy road to the ruins of Sinister Bend.

"Where are we going anyway?"

"You'll see," he says.

It's only about a two-mile walk, but it feels like we're descending into one of the outer rings of Hades. We go down the hill and arrive at the Bend, the treacherous pile of rocks in the river that used to beach boats and gave the town its name— the very spot where I imagine Ptan Teca went for his last swim.

After crossing the river by the arched bridge with a bunch of "Danger" and "Do Not Enter" signs, we bear east, taking a gentle rise to the higher part of the town—the part that was only regularly flooded, and not completely claimed by the lake. There's garbage and debris strewn about, and rotten sewage smells fill the air. Only the occasional patch of cement in the mud suggests our path used to be an actual road.

When my dad was a little kid, he tells me, it was still

possible to find arrowheads and other artifacts in the mud around Sinister Bend. Kids would go with their classes to find them and learn about the history of the region.

Now another civilization has sunk into the mud. Perhaps future school groups will sort through the remains of Sinister Bend, looking for artifacts from the 1980s. I imagine a museum case full of Wham! records, armless Cabbage Patch dolls, and "Reelect Reagan" buttons.

It's eerily quiet, and neither of us talks as we walk past the sagging houses and moldy buildings, curious what the buildings might have once been. A coffee shop? A beauty salon? I wonder what became of the people who lived in those houses, and what they left behind. Their houses must be filled with their former belongings, rotten and decayed and tossed about by the floodwaters.

The road narrows, and it seems to get darker as the hills on either side become steeper. We walk on into the shadows. The houses here are bigger. Of course, they are just as broken down and lifeless as the other houses, but this used to be the nicer part of Sinister Bend.

"Nearly there," says Sturgis. We reach the end of the path at a clearing where the sun breaks through the hills and shines brightly. We cross what used to be the massive lawn of a large house. Off to the right, some kids are laughing and hollering. They have lines drawn in the dirt and are playing sandlot baseball, with five or six kids on a side. P.J. is there and a few other kids I recognize from Sutton Little League.

Out of the front door comes Peter, smiling and offering his hand.

"Roy, it's good to see you," he says.

"What—why are the Pirates practicing here?"

"We're not the Pirates anymore," he says. "We're the Sinister Bend team now."

"You moved the whole team to a ruined town?"

"We don't live here. We just practice here. We wanted it to be official."

"Official?"

"Officially Sinister Bend. So we can play the rematch."

"Just practicing here once or twice doesn't make your team Sinister Bend." I don't know what he's trying to prove, just slapping a Sinister Bend sticker on a Sutton team that's always going to the play-offs.

"The Pirates are all kids from Sinister Bend," he explains. "Their families are originally from Sinister Bend anyway. The families that ended up in Sutton, we keep in touch with each other. We wanted to have a team ready for when it finally stopped raining."

I gulp once or twice. While most of the kids in Moundville are learning the game all over again, Sinister Bend has a team of ringers just waiting to beat the snot out of us. I have to hand it to them. They take their baseball pretty seriously.

"Wow, that's c—commitment." I'd started to say "crazy," which is a better word for it.

"We can play on Labor Day," Peter says cheerfully, like

it's all in fun. "It'll be like the old days, right? Everyone will have the day off."

"What's the hurry? We barely have a team ourselves. We could even play next year."

"This is when we're supposed to play," Peter replies seriously, so low only I can hear. "That's why the rain stopped. He was waiting for the right moment. This is it." I guess that "he" is Ptan Teca, the old ghost who's got nothing better to do than fix baseball games.

Peter raises his voice again. "We can have a picnic and fireworks. It's not the Fourth of July, but it's almost as good."

"Sounds great," I lie. Then I think, Maybe it won't be so bad. So what if the Pirates were perennial champs? With Sturgis pitching for us, it would be a close game. We could get lucky and score a couple of runs. Who knows? Maybe we'd surprise them.

Sturgis turns to watch the other boys. They're ignoring us, continuing with their game.

He pulls out a yellow baseball cap that's been scrunched up and stuffed in his back pocket, hidden under his shirt. It's tattered at the edges and looks older than him. He shakes out the wrinkles and puts it on, pulling the brim down to shade his eyes.

The hat has *SB* stitched on it. It's an old-school Sinister Bend cap. I wonder how old it is.

"I'll be on their team, of course," he says.

⚾ ⚾ ⚾

As far as anyone knows, it's a friendly rivalry and we're all good sports. I even stay for lunch. Peter grills up a few dozen hot dogs, his wife brings out a huge bowl of potato salad and some big bottles of soda, and we have a little barbecue.

While we eat, Peter introduces the Sinister Bend team. The names and faces blur for me, and it takes a second to sink in that my friend Ty is also on their team. When he's introduced, he just nods, like we've never met.

Sturgis is at the far side of the table, acting aloof. He talks a bit to the other kids but barely talks to me. If he thinks we're still friends, he's wrong. I don't know if he's playing for Sinister Bend out of loyalty or just because he's mad at me for dissing his dad. Either way, I taught him to pitch, and I stuck up for him, and I think it's pretty low to go slinking off in the night to join another team.

I never cared much about winning. I just like the game. But now I realize with a burning in my stomach that I *must beat* Sturgis. It's not just about Moundville beating Sinister Bend, but me personally beating him. I want to pound his fastball right back at him, knock it right over his head and out of the ballpark, taking his stupid baseball cap with it.

That's how I feel, but to watch me, you'd think I was at a wedding reception. I'm all smiles and pleased to meetcha and pass the potato salad. I have my game face on.

Peter offers us a ride after lunch, but I decide to walk. Sturgis decides to walk, too. And so I set out for home, quietly fuming, with Sturgis trailing about ten paces back. Once, I stop to let him catch up. He pauses to stamp some of the mud off his shoes and doesn't stop until I resume walking myself.

Eventually, I turn around and face him.

"Well?"

"Well what?"

"Do you want to talk about this?"

"What is there to talk about?" He tries to walk past me, and I push him in the chest.

"You being a traitor."

He shrugs. "I'm a free agent."

"I helped you learn how to pitch," I remind him.

"I don't need your stupid junkball to win. I'll throw nothin' but fastballs and strike you babies out." He's not playing it cool anymore. I can see his face turning red, at least where it isn't scarred.

"Like to see you sneak one past me." I poke him in the chest again.

"It won't just go past you. It'll go *through* you," he says.

"What the heck does that mean?"

"It means you're not just getting fastballs, Roy. You're getting fastballs right in your ear hole."

"You just try. I'll rip that fake ear off your head and cram it down your throat."

"That'll be hard to do when you're unconscious."

"That's all you can do, huh? Throw things at people? Like crab apples. I'm sure your dad will be real proud."

"Yesterday you put down my dad, and now you make fun of my ear. You really hit below the belt, don't you?"

"Better than being a lousy traitor."

"Who did I betray, huh? You?"

"The team. All of us."

"Those kids don't even like me," he says.

"It's not true," I say lamely. It is kind of true. The other guys like having Sturgis on their team, but I don't think they like Sturgis.

"You never really tried to make them like you," I remind him. "You yell at them all the time, and you sulked when you got taken out of a game, and . . ." I try to think of his other crimes. "You plunked David that time."

"You can't make guys like you," he says. "All you can do is strike them out."

"Oh, right."

"Or plug 'em," he says. He mimes a throw and makes a little whistling noise like a missile flying. "Kaboom!" He throws up his hands, his long fingers splayed out all over. "Keep your chin up, Roy," he says, and marches on ahead toward home.

The rumors take flight and ride on the wind back to Moundville. By the time we get to town, there is already a buzz in the air and whispers on the street. The rematch is on! Moundville and Sinister Bend will play! Pedestrians whisper as we pass by and point us out to their friends. Cars slow down so people can get a look at us. I wonder if it's my imagination, but when a car beeps its horn, it's followed by another and another. A few people on the sidewalk clap a little as we pass. Pretty soon, there's so much honking and clapping it sounds like a parade of geese and trained seals is marching through town.

Nobody is more excited than my dad.

"You know I can't pick sides," he says. "I have to stay impartial. So I'm just rooting for both teams to do well. Boy, this will be so great for the town, won't it? And great for my business. Every person in town will see that sign on the outfield fence and ask about it, and the word will go around that we put down the grass, that we're the ones who brought baseball back to Moundville. And they'll think, You know, we could use a new lawn and a patio or maybe a pergola. Plus, I can get a concession stand. T-shirts, even."

"Sounds good, Dad."

I'm glad he can make a profit out of my impending disgrace.

On Tuesday morning, the ballpark is a madhouse. We had occasional onlookers before, but now there's an actual crowd. They hoot and holler at us as we gather at the mound for a short team conference.

"You've probably all heard the rumors by now," I announce.

"I hear we're playing Sinister Bend next week," says Steve.

"Six days, actually."

"And Sturgis has quit the team." Shannon sounds hoarse. "Is that true?"

"He's playing for the Sinister Bend team now," I admit.

"No way!" Kazuo reels in disbelief.

Apparently, not everyone has heard the rumors.

"What's up with that?" says Rita furiously. "I ought to . . ." She can't think of what she ought to do. I assume it's something violent.

"No way we can win now," says Carlos.

"Never liked that guy anyway," says Miggy casually.

"Benedict Arnold," says Steve bitterly.

"Maybe if we go back to him and apologize for . . . for whatever he thinks we did?" suggests Shannon.

"It's not about us," I tell her. "He's just loyal to Sinister Bend."

"I don't understand!" says Shannon.

"I *hate* Sinister Bend," says Tim.

They continue to complain and commiserate for several minutes, until Kazuo ends it with a question.

"Who's pitching for us?"

Everyone is quiet, then looks at Rita. Rita looks at me in fright—either because she might not be the starting pitcher or because she might be. It's hard to say.

"I don't know yet," I tell them.

"Is there any way we can win?" asks Carlos.

"I don't know," I tell him. "Probably not."

"Do we have to play at all?" asks Shannon.

"You're darn right we have to play!" says Tim. "It's Sinister Bend!"

"So what?" Shannon shrugs.

"We shouldn't have out-of-towners on the team," he grumbles. "They don't understand."

"Well, are we going to practice, or are we just going to complain?" says David in disgust. He heads out to first base. "Who's batting?" We look at him in disbelief.

"I'll bat," says Rita. "Just throw me some slow, fat pitches and I'll pretend they're Sturgis's head."

"I can pitch a little," says Kazuo. "I can pitch BP anyway."

Pretty soon we're all in position and playing ball.

We run the drill the usual way, trying to get batting practice and fielding practice in by taking turns at the plate and moving around the field to fill in the gaps.

The crowd of spectators mostly stays out of our way, but they also give us plenty of unsolicited advice.

"Keep your wrists together!" a fellow shouts while David is batting. David whiffs on the first pitch from Kazuo. It's embarrassing because Kazuo is lobbing grapefruits at him.

"Open up your stance!" shouts another. David whiffs again.

"Go with the pitch!" shouts the first fellow. David swings late and barely nicks the ball.

"Go the other way!" shouts the second. David swings

early and pops the ball foul. It's fielded by an onlooker, who tosses it back to Kazuo.

"Try changing your arm angle," he tells Kazuo. "You want your arm to be at two o'clock."

"I can't concentrate!" David complains, throwing the bat on the ground.

"Get used to it," I tell him. "It'll be a lot worse on game day."

New kids show up, too, wanting to play. I have to try them out, just in case one is a brilliant pitcher. None of them are, and I have to tell most of them to wait until next year—they don't know how to play, and we don't have time to teach them.

We do keep one kid. He's no bigger than a peanut and knows about two words of English. He's got a glove so old it might have been used by George Wright.

"Baseball," he tells me, nodding happily at the diamond.

"Do you have any experience?"

"Search me," he says, smiling and nodding enthusiastically.

"Do you know what position you want to play?" I ask.

"Search me," he says again, with the same nod.

"Third base?" I point to the base. "Er, *beso tres?*"

"*Sí!*"

He runs out there and proves within minutes that he was born to play the hot corner. What he lacks in height, he makes up for with enthusiasm and the ability to jump about four feet in the air. He also knows the fundamentals and barks orders and instructions to the other fielders—mostly in Spanish, but he seems to know what he's talking about.

"What's your name?" David wants to know.

"Search me," the boy tells him with a nod.

"Pleased to meet you, Google," says David. Pretty soon we're all calling him Google, even after Miggy figures out that the kid's real name is Félix.

"He says he's from Miami," says Miggy.

"I thought they spoke English in Miami," says Steve.

"Search me," says Google, followed by a string of Spanish.

"He's from Cuba by way of Miami," Miggy corrects himself.

"How does anyone come from Cuba?" asks David. "I thought they didn't allow it."

Miggy puts the question to Google in Spanish, but Google just shrugs.

"Search me," he says.

"He says it's a long story," says Miggy.

Chapter 19

With good leather at third base, I move Miggy to left field, where he gets into less trouble, and demote Carlos to batboy. Carlos doesn't mind, so long as he can hang out with the team.

Google takes Carlos under his wing, explaining the duties of a batboy in elaborate detail—in Spanish, of course.

"He's kind of bossy," Carlos tells me. "He sure knows a lot about baseball, though."

Finding a third baseman and getting a minor upgrade in left field don't make up for losing our pitcher. Steve says he can handle it, but I'm not sure he can, and I don't want to lose him at shortstop. I think the only thing we can do is teach Rita how to throw a fastball.

"Your screwball will be more effective if you can set it up with a fastball," I explain to her. It's late Wednesday afternoon, which gives her about four days to develop a skill guys spend ten years learning. The pressure takes all the romance out of holding her hand, trying to show her the right grip.

"I told you, I can't throw straight," she says.

"If you can just straighten out a little bit, you'll be okay," I tell her. "Try overthrowing it a bit."

She throws some balls to me, but even when she straightens them out, she can't get any smoke on them. I begin to wonder if Kazuo should pitch, with Google at second base and Miggy back at third. The thought doesn't thrill me. I only think of Kazuo because he can pitch left-handed.

Rita is rearing back to try again when a stocky guy, about thirty-five years old, comes marching in and grabs the ball from her.

"Let me demonstrate," he says. He shows her a four-seam grip and starts to say something.

"Thanks, but we've got it under control," I tell him.

"No, no you don't," he tells me. "If she throws like that, she'll get shelled." He turns back to Rita, sticking the baseball in her face.

"Excuse me, sir." She backs up a few paces.

"Come on, just let me show you a four-seamer. I want us to win this thing," he says. He starts modeling the pitch, telling her to look at how he anchors his feet and keeps his elbow in and finds the balance point and turns his hand over.

"Really, sir, we appreciate it, but we need to have focus," I tell him.

"Listen, kid," he says, "I don't know who put you in charge, but I've seen you kids practicing, and you'll get destroyed. You got no pitching."

"The team put me in charge," I tell him.

"Your pitcher's going to get shelled if she throws like that."

"Hey, buddy, what's the problem?" A thick hand takes the man by the elbow, and another takes the baseball from him.

It's Frank. Right behind him is Lou.

218

"I was just trying to help," the man says meekly.

"The kid told you he's got it under control," says Frank.

"They're going to lose!" the man shouts. He turns to the crowd, looking for support.

"Hey, I believe in these kids," says Lou. "Are you saying that you don't?" He says it more to the crowd than to the man.

It's a short battle for public support, won by Lou.

"Horn out, jerk!"

"Leave the kids alone!"

"Let them practice."

"Mind your own business, chump!"

The group cheers when the man finally backs off the field, looking glum.

"Thanks," I say to Frank and Lou.

"Hey, no problem, Roy. I guess Bobby there just wants to relive his glory days."

"Bobby? You know that guy?"

"That's Bobby Fitz. He used to play ball, you know."

I remember the boy on the old video who mows down the opposition in the top of the first but is injured trying to take an extra base. "My dad says he's the best pitcher Moundville ever had."

"Great hitter, too," adds Lou. "Almost a better hitter than he was a pitcher."

"Are you kidding? He had an ERA in the decimals." Frank shakes his head at Lou's ignorance.

"I did say 'almost,'" Lou protests.

"He could steal bases, too," says Frank. "He was an all-around great player. Had all the tools. Should have gone pro. Problem was, you know, the nagging injuries."

"And the fact he maxed out at five foot six." Lou crouches down to illustrate. "Not too many pros that size."

"And that was him?" I can't believe it. My dad talks about him all the time. They used to be good friends. I never met him, though.

"That's the guy. If he's acting like a jerk, it's just because he's really fanatical about Moundville baseball."

"Just a sec!" I take off in a sprint and chase the balding man about a block and a half. He's just getting into his car, maybe heading back to his insurance job in Sutton.

"Hey, Mr. Fitz!"

"Call me Bobby."

"Can you teach Rita how to throw a fastball?"

"That's what I was trying to do."

We walk back to the field, and he picks up where he left off. I don't know what the magic is, but pretty soon Rita is throwing straight. Not fast, but for now I'll settle for a straightball.

It's lonely at home. My dad and Sturgis are talking shop and cooking something together in the kitchen. Sturgis proves to have the same improvisational flair. Under my dad's tutelage, he invents the enchilada stew.

Over dinner, my dad tells us he found a place in Sutton

where he can rent a food service tent and a big grill. "I can get everything I need for the game," he says cheerfully.

"Um, what are you going to cook?" I ask nervously.

"Just hot dogs and stuff."

I'm relieved. Even my dad can't mess up hot dogs that much.

"So what's in this?" I ask a few minutes later, taking a forkful of stew and looking skeptically at a piece of meat. "Is it *rabbit meat*?" I give Sturgis a hard, squinty look I hope is menacing.

"No, it's chicken," my dad says, confused.

Sturgis just squints back at me. "There's beans in it, too," he says. "You *love* beans, don't you, Roy?"

"Huh?" my dad says. "I'd say Roy is ambivalent about beans."

"Oh, I bet he'd like to feast on beans," says Sturgis.

When my dad isn't looking, he mimes a pitch, then a batter getting hit in the ribs. "Oof," he mouths, then pantomimes a man falling dead, his tongue poking out of his mouth. It's pretty childish.

I wake up long before Sturgis on Thursday morning. Sleep has become more and more elusive for me. I get dressed in the dark and go to the kitchen. Yogi pads after me, quietly meowing for breakfast. I give him some, although he's sure to get a second helping when the others wake up.

We have three days until the game. We can't even

practice tomorrow because they're installing bleachers. I don't see how we can possibly be ready. Everything we've done as a team has revolved around Sturgis being a lights-out pitcher.

I turn on the TV, muted, to catch the sports scores. The blue screen comes on for the DVD player, and instead of flipping the switch to TV, I use the universal remote to turn on the DVD. I'm curious what someone's been watching.

It's the same old DVD of the game from twenty years ago. My dad must have been watching it, reliving his defining moment. There's Bobby Fitz cruising through the first inning, and there's the Sinister Bend pitcher warming up, with the familiar sneer and hair in his eyes.

The familiar sneer.

In English class, we learned the word "epiphany." I forget what the story was about, but an epiphany is when a guy is going about his business and *bam*, he has a realization about something. I think in the story, the guy suddenly realized he didn't believe in God. Or maybe he realized he *did* believe in God. It doesn't matter.

What matters is that I have an epiphany, right in the middle of a bowl of cereal, two seconds before I flip over to the sports news channel for the ticker with last night's baseball scores.

The epiphany is this: The mean kid on the mound is Carey Nye. That battered baseball cap Sturgis wears is his father's old cap. Sturgis doesn't want to beat Moundville for Sinister Bend. He wants to do it for his old man.

It must have been Sturgis, not my dad, who stayed up

222

late watching that DVD. I imagine him watching that fatal last pitch over and over, his teeth grinding as he vows revenge. Never mind that my dad has taken him in and even bought him his baseball glove.

Well, that's his prerogative.

I venture out, heading for the ballpark, as if extra hours by myself can make any kind of difference.

That morning at the ballpark, a woman parks a rented car illegally, brushes past the crowd, and makes her way to the bullpen, where Bobby is helping Rita with the fastball. She greets Bobby Fitz with a familiar hug.

"He's got a pretty cute wife," says Steve.

"That's not his wife. I think it's my mom," I tell him. Steve's mouth drops open.

"I just haven't seen her in so long," he tries to explain as I walk slowly to the bullpen, taking off my mask.

"Hi, Roy," my mom says.

"Hey."

She gives me a hug and a peck on the cheek. "I can barely get my arms around you with this thing," she says, tapping the chest protector. "And you're so big now!"

"That's what happens," I tell her.

"So I hear you're the big man out here," she says.

"Yeah, I'm captain." I mean it to be matter-of-fact but come off sounding like a small boy trying to impress his mommy. I'm surprised she doesn't give me a cookie. Or maybe I'm just self-conscious because Rita is looking on.

"Well," my mom says, "I thought I would come see your big game."

"You know about that, huh?"

"Word gets around. I would have been here sooner, but I was in Barcelona. I took the whole weekend off and came straight here."

So that's how big this game is. Long-lost relatives fly in from Mediterranean ports, arriving just in time to watch us lose.

"Mom's here," I tell my father that evening as I try to find an entry point to a cabbage thing that might have been Sturgis's idea. My dad has done some awful things as a cook, but he's never made me eat cabbage before. Now I've got a massive raw cabbage leaf on my plate, folded and tied around a mysterious lump.

"Is she?" he says, trying to act casual. He's poking at his thing with a fork. Sturgis has already eaten his and taken off somewhere, probably with his new baseball friends.

"She seemed pretty happy to see Bobby Fitz," I tell him.

"Well, we used to all be friends," he explains.

"Including you and Carey Nye?" I ask.

"Sure, a little." He goes after his cabbage leaf with a knife. A cascade of minced chicken, celery, carrots, and red pepper flakes spills out. I hack at my own cabbage thing until I get at the filling. I take a bite. It's not bad, actually.

"So you know Sturgis's dad?"

He takes a long time to chew and swallow. "It sounds like maybe you've done some sleuthing."

"Not really. I just figured out stuff."

"Well, the fact is . . ." He takes a deep breath, bracing himself. "Carey used to work for me. He worked *with* me, I should say. I wasn't the boss or anything back then. We were just a couple of guys doing odd jobs together, you see."

"It seems kind of weird, that you'd be friends, after that game and everything."

"Well, that was only baseball, for one thing," my dad says. "Carey was a hard worker, and putting up those rain systems, you really need two sets of hands, and it made sense for us to do it together."

"Why him, though? You must have had other buddies. What about Bobby Fitz?"

"Roy, Carey was practically family. He was engaged to Evie." Aunt Evelyn is little more than a rumor to me. She's the one who died in a car accident. I was a baby at the time. I don't even remember meeting her. My dad hardly ever talks about her.

"They met in high school," he says, "and that was that. My sister was crazy about him. They got serious fast. Maybe it had to do with our dad not being around. I needed help and Carey needed work, so . . ." He shrugs.

"Well, I guess it's not a big deal," I say. "So did they like break up or something? When he went off to be a baseball player?"

My father takes a long, deep breath. "Roy . . ." He looks at me, and suddenly I get it.

"They *were* married?"

"Yes."

"So Sturgis is . . ."

"My nephew. Your cousin. We're his next of kin. That's why he's here. I never signed up for foster parenting."

"Why didn't I know him when we were little?"

"Carey was always a bit of a bully, and when he went into pro ball, he got worse. You give the wrong kind of guy a little money, and it ruins him. He was arrogant, and he wasn't good to my sister, and I just didn't like him much. We drifted apart. That's all. It happens."

"Me and Sturgis could have hung out, though." I imagine a pint-sized Sturgis lobbing Nerf balls at me. "We could have always been buddies."

"I'm sorry," he says. "You probably would have been good for each other."

"So why didn't you tell me all that? At least, when Sturgis moved in."

"I don't know," he says. "I meant to. I guess there's just a lot of old scabs I didn't want to pick at. Like losing Evie." He looks forlornly at his cold supper like he might start blubbering. I decide against making him pick at that scab any more.

Chapter **20**

I meet Miggy and Google at the ballpark on Friday. We can't practice, but we have other plans. Carlos, as always, is in tow.

"Let's go," I tell them.

"*Vamos*," says Miggy, and the four of us start walking through town.

"Sinister Bend stinks!" someone screams at us as we walk by the town hall. A few other drivers are happy just to honk their horns. I also notice a bedsheet has been carelessly hung from the water tower, spray-painted in red: "Go, Mudville Nine!"

We walk to the brink of the hill heading down to Sinister Bend. Miggy and Carlos translate for me, explaining the situation to Google. We need him to be our scout, Miggy tells him, because he's the only player Sturgis and P.J. don't know. He is to go join the Sinister Bend team for the morning. If they don't let him play, he should just watch. He'll come back after a couple of hours and tell Miggy everything, and Miggy will tell me. What are the team's strengths? What are its weaknesses? How many right- and left-handed batters do they have?

I give him directions to where the Sinister Bend team plays, and he hurries off. In the meantime, the three of us toss a ball around.

"We don't live far from here," says Miggy after about an hour. "I could go get lunch and come back. I'll make sandwiches for everyone."

That sounds good to me. Miggy trots off, and Carlos waits with me.

"You guys are pretty close, eh?"

"Of course," he says. "We're brothers. Like you and the mean boy."

"We're not brothers."

A moment later, we hear shouts and footsteps. Google is flying up the road toward us. He's crying, and yelling in Spanish.

Carlos shouts back in Spanish and runs to meet him. They go back and forth for a while, Google talking excitedly and Carlos trying to calm him down.

"He says they're chasing him," Carlos says. He looks down the hill, searching for someone, and shakes his head. He talks to Google. "I just told him there's nobody there," he says.

Google talks some more and rubs his head. There is already a knot growing on it.

"He says they let him play," says Carlos, "but then . . ."

"I think I can guess what happened," I say.

The moment Sturgis walks in, I jab him in the chest and back him up to the door.

"What's with you?" he asks.

"You plugged Google!" I say.

"Who?"

"You hit our player. In the head!"

"He was a spy," he says calmly.

"He wasn't a spy, he was a scout. It's part of the game," I tell him. "And, by the way, you and P.J. know everything about our team, so why shouldn't we know anything about yours?"

"We don't need any information about your team," he says. "Do you think we're breaking down each batter, figuring out how to pitch you and how to play you? That's a laugh. I can strike every one of you out, and that's all I need to do."

"If you're so sure, what do you care if we send a scout over?"

"Because it's dirty business," he says. "That's all."

"It's part of the game," I tell him. "Anyway, you never throw at a guy's head. Never!"

"Ah, I just wanted to scare him," he says casually.

"You could have seriously hurt him."

"It was just a junkball. About a three."

"The next time you hit someone, I'll flatten you."

"You're the one I'll plunk first," he mutters. "Brace yourself for a ten, Roy. A twenty, even."

"Yeah? Well, I'll throw the ball right back at you," I tell him. "I'll do a little head-hunting of my own. See how you like it."

"Hey, hey," says my dad, coming out of the office. "What's going on?"

"Nothing," I say. "Just a little smack talk."

"Settle it on the ball field, okay?"

"Oh, that's what I plan to do," says Sturgis with a sly grin.

Much later, when we're supposed to be sleeping, I shake Sturgis awake.

"Did you know that we're related?" I ask him.

"Yeah. We're cousins."

"Why didn't you tell me?"

"I thought you knew."

"Sure you did. That's why you call my dad Uncle Bill all the time."

"Well, I'm sorry. Are you going to flatten me now?" He's still fuming about how I threatened him.

"You should've told me. I never lied to you."

"You lied to me about Yogi."

"What are you talking about?"

"You told me he had an accident and that was how he lost his tail. Well, I looked it up on the Internet, and Manx cats just come like that."

"I didn't lie exactly," I sputter. "I just didn't go out of my way to tell you the truth."

"Well, same here."

"That's different." I try to think of a good reason why it's different.

"Can I go back to sleep now?"

"I guess," I tell him. "I don't care anyway."

He's out cold in seconds. The secret-keeping traitor sleeps like a baby. Meanwhile, me and my clean conscience toss and turn.

There are big cardboard boxes waiting in the dugout on Sunday morning.

In the boxes are new uniforms. They're white with silver and gold pinstripes, and the caps have the letter M in bold, fancy script. The logo of the realty company where Steve's mom works is sewn on the sleeves. I guess that takes the mystery out of who paid for them.

"These are awesome," I tell Steve.

"She saw everything your dad did and wanted to do her part." He grins, and I know he's thinking the same thing as me. She wanted her fair share of the publicity.

We don't have proper locker rooms yet, but the pool hall across the street lets everyone change in the back room. The girls go first, then us.

"We look like a real baseball team!" says David after he changes.

"I sure hope we can play like one," I reply.

We proceed not to. Suddenly everyone on the team is tripping over ground balls in the field and striking out at the plate. As morning turns to afternoon, we just get worse. The usual crowd of spectators are quiet, most of them shaking their heads in misery. However, a few Sinister Bend supporters hang around to heckle.

I knew the Sinister Bend team had some good players, but I was hoping there were a few weaknesses we could exploit. No such luck. Google tells me (with Miggy translating) that the Sinister Bend team is tough all the way through the order. They can hit the ball, and they play good defense. With Sturgis pitching, they'll be hard to beat. All the more reason to wince with every misstep and blunder as we practice.

When Anthony bounces a ball over the pitcher's mound and into center field, though, I lose my temper.

"No, no, no!" I shout. "That should have been a double-play ball, not a double! What are you doing, Rita? You're not done with the play after you pitch. You have to field your position!"

"It was over my head."

"You can reach for it," I tell her. "It wasn't that high. If you can't catch it, at least knock it down. And, Kaz, why aren't you backing her up?"

"I didn't know I was supposed to."

"This is ridiculous! We're playing tomorrow, and we're not even close to ready."

"We're trying, Captain," says Rita.

"I know, I know," I say. "But we don't get any outs for trying. We have to execute."

"We've only been playing a few weeks," says Kazuo. "We've come a long way, all things considered."

"I know. I just feel like we're moving backward." I look around at everyone. A couple of guys lower their heads, just like I'm a real coach hollering at them.

"Look, I don't care if they beat us. I just don't want to beat ourselves." It's a lie, of course; I do care if they beat us. It would be worse if we made it easy on them, though. "Steve, that means no hotdogging. You're not Ozzie Smith. Kazuo, that means throwing to the right base. Rita, that means not being afraid of the ball when it comes back at you. Google, that means—never mind, you're perfect."

"Search me," he says with a grin.

"Shannon, that means looking in for signs. I might need to shade you over. Look on every pitch. I mean it. You get bored out there and stop paying attention. Miggy and Tim, do what Shannon tells you. And keep the ball in front of you, Miggy. Don't overrun it."

"Yeah, yeah," he says.

"Look, Roy," says Bobby, coming out. "I wonder if I can talk to you a second."

He takes me aside and talks in a low voice.

"Look at your team."

I look at them, scuffling around in the dirt, and feel queasy.

"We'll never be ready," I say, shaking my head.

"I think maybe you kids need some time off. You're not going to become major leaguers this afternoon, so why not call it a day and come in fresh tomorrow?"

"I guess you're right," I say. The truth is, I need the break more than anyone. I'm beat.

"All right," I announce, heading back to the group. "We're taking the rest of the day off. Take it easy and get a good night's sleep. We have a baseball game to play tomorrow."

The team looks sort of confused at first, then relieved.

"All right, Captain, see you tomorrow," says Rita with a friendly tap on the back.

They slowly scatter, while the most die-hard fans offer a smattering of applause, yelling "Let's go get 'em!" and junk like that.

I have a hard time leaving the field. I just look out at the grass, the new bleachers, and the scoreboard. I think about all the team captains who've stood here the day before the big game—none of them recently, of course—each one nervous and excited for the next day. Some might have felt they had a chance. Others probably felt hopeless, as I do. I remember Peter's stories about how it just felt like the Moundville team was fated to lose.

"We'll get creamed," I say to Bobby.

"Then you'll be part of a long tradition of Moundville baseball," he says.

I notice my mother is in the stands after everyone else has wandered off.

"I've been wondering what you're up to," I tell her. I haven't seen her since the first time she came to practice.

"I didn't want to be a distraction," she says. "I know how it is."

"Yeah."

"Well, maybe we can catch up now? I'll buy you a soda and a sandwich."

"Sure." I'm not too comfortable with it but can't see any way around it. Besides, I'm hungry.

We pop into the downtown diner. As soon as I walk in, people are elbowing each other and pointing me out. The booths are all taken, but some people vacate theirs and let us sit down.

"Good luck tomorrow, Roy," they tell me.

The waitress rushes over to clear the table for us.

"What can I get you, champ?" she asks.

I order a chili dog with fries and a root beer.

"Lots of onions on the chili dog," I tell the waitress.

"You got it, champ."

My mother just gets a Diet Coke.

"Lot of people rooting for you," my mom says with a smile as the waitress runs off to put in our order.

"Sure," I say.

"Your father among them," she says. "I hear he rebuilt the ballpark, just so he could see you play. He wants you to win, Roy."

"He's been acting kind of neutral," I tell her. "Since Sturgis is on the other team, he's trying to be impartial."

"Deep down inside, your dad is a Moundville boy," she says. "This place brings out the hero in him."

"You mean his defining moment?" I ask.

"What?"

I remind her how his base hit forced a rain delay, saving Moundville from a horrible defeat, even if it didn't get them a win.

"I remember it well," she says. "He was up there forever. I couldn't help but love him, the way he fought off all those pitches. It was so heroic. Even though part of me died when he got that hit, I was proud of him."

"Part of you died?"

"I was rooting for Sinister Bend, silly. I'm from Sinister Bend."

"Oh, right." I sort of knew that but forgot. "What about tomorrow?" I ask her. "Who are you rooting for?"

"Now that's a chili dog!" She changes the subject, but when I see the plate, I understand. They've completely drowned the dog in chili, and there's so much chopped onion piled on, it looks like a ski slope. There's also shredded cheese and jalapeño peppers and a couple of handfuls of Fritos thrown in for good measure. As the waitress puts it down, the whole crew gathers around her and cheers. It's like birthday cake with no candles.

"I'm a lucky girl," my mom says. "I'm on a date with the biggest hero in town."

"Please don't say weird things like that," I ask her as I grab the mustard from the end of the table.

"You need mustard, too?"

"It's not a hot dog without mustard." I sploosh it on.

For a while, I focus on my hot dog and root beer. My mother sips her Coke and steals a couple of my fries, dipping them in the wildly excessive chili and cheese on my plate. Meanwhile, I discover there are *two* frankfurters hiding under the mess of toppings. It's absolutely the best meal I've ever had.

"Your father might think life is about defining moments,"

my mom says, "but it's not. It's about what you do day to day. He's not a hero because of what he did in that game. He's a hero because of what he did after."

I look at her blankly.

"Roy, your father helped save this town," she says. "He found a way to save people's homes and keep them here."

"It's just his job," I tell her.

"Then it's all the more heroic," she says. "He could have chased his own dreams, but he stayed behind and did what he had to do."

I sip my root beer and scoop up some chili dog drippings with a French fry. My silence says more than enough.

"Oh," she says sadly. "I didn't, did I? Roy, I was just a kid when I got married. Barely out of high school. It was always raining, and I was really unhappy. I guess I just needed to leave, to save myself."

"It's okay," I tell her. I don't sound like I mean it, but then, I don't mean it.

"I knew your father would raise you right, and he did."

"I guess," I tell her.

"He's doing great with Sturgis, too," she says.

"I guess," I say again. "He doesn't drag him to dogfights anyway."

"What on earth are you talking about?"

I recount the story about the dogfight in Sutton, but it sounds lame even to me. I remember Rita saying it sounded made up. It probably is, I realize.

"Roy, Sturgis was hurt in the same car accident that killed his mother. Carey was drunk and insisted on driving home from some party, wherever they were that night. He crashed into another car. It hit the passenger side, and Evelyn, your aunt . . . she died immediately, and Sturgis was badly hurt by shattered glass. Carey wasn't hurt at all. They found him on the highway, running, scared out of his mind, and so drunk he couldn't remember any of it later."

So maybe Sturgis had scabs of his own he didn't want to pick at. I suddenly feel queasy and claustrophobic. I want to be doing anything other than talking to my mother in a crowded diner. I'd rather be digging ditches in the rain.

"I need to go," I tell her.

"You'll be okay?"

"Why would I not be okay?" I ask her. It's not her business to ask anyway, I think. It's not like she can check in every few years and buy me a chili dog and ask me if everything is okay.

I brush by the people in the diner, nodding politely, not hearing whatever they shout in my ear. I go out the door, across the street, and back to the outfield grass Sturgis and I laid out with our own hands. I go to the dugout and lie down on the brand-new bench. I pull my cap low over my eyes and sink down until I'm invisible.

So it wasn't a wolf that left a mark on Sturgis, I think. It was his dad.

⚾ ⚾ ⚾

"What's going on with Roy?" someone asks.

"Search me," says another voice.

I'm shaken awake by Miggy. He's with Google and Anthony and, of course, his shadow, Carlos. I sit up and rub my eyes.

"We want to practice," he says.

"What time is it?"

"Evening." He shrugs. I see the shadows are getting longer in the outfield.

"Will you pitch batting practice?" Miggy asks. "Just an hour or so?"

"Nah," I tell them. "If you can't hit now, one more hour's not going to help."

Miggy nods and speaks a bit to the other boys in Spanish. Google answers, and Miggy laughs.

"He says he wants practice dodging bullets," he explains.

"We'll probably need that," I agree.

"We're going to get killed, aren't we?" asks Carlos.

"Probably," I admit.

Google says something in Spanish again, and Miggy translates.

"He says he can't wait," he tells me.

I head home, skip supper (I'm still pretty full from lunch), and go to bed early. Exhaustion wins out over insomnia, and I finally get a good night's sleep.

I do have bad dreams, though. In one, I oversleep and show up late to the game. When I get there, we're already trailing by a score of twenty-three to nothing, and the Sinister Bend team is in full Dakota war dress, looking like extras from an old Western. In another, my mom stands up in the bleachers, just like the woman in *The Natural*. Sturgis throws a ball at her and knocks her head clean off. The crowd cheers, and the umpire hands him a giant stuffed panda.

I blame the bad dreams on stress and too much chili dog.

When I wake up, Sturgis is long gone. So is my dad. Somebody's scrawled "Good luck!" on the marker board and drawn a smiley face in a baseball cap. Either it's my dad and he means it or it's Sturgis and he's being sarcastic.

Chapter **21**

I can smell burned frankfurter two blocks before I get to the ballpark, and I figure my dad has already set up his hot dog tent. I hope he's just testing out the equipment and not selling whatever it is I smell to customers.

He gives me a friendly wave as I walk by.

People begin to fill the bleachers as we practice. They clap and chatter as we take batting practice and shag fly balls. The fielding warm-up is crisp and steady. Maybe Bobby Fitz was right. We just needed a day off.

The Sinister Bend team shows up an hour later. They're wearing their Pirates uniforms and new yellow caps with *SB* drawn on the front, the *S* hooking the *B*. No two are the same. Most of the logos are misshapen or out of proportion. Sturgis still wears his old cap.

"Hey, let's get off the field so those guys can warm up," I tell my team. We gather our stuff and head for the dugout.

I pass Sturgis as he heads out on the field.

"Hey, Coz," I say, offering a hand.

He trots by me without a word, his game face on.

A few of us visit the hot dog tent while the Sinister Bend team gets ready. My dad is grilling up hot dogs by the dozen.

"Free hot dogs for players!" he announces, and starts lining up the counter with paper baskets, each with a hot dog, a little pile of chips, and a dill pickle. We all take one, and a couple of us take two. Not even my dad can mess up hot dogs that much, even if he does offer people sliced olives and crushed pineapple as optional toppings.

"Use both," he tells us. "I call it the Caribbean!"

My stomach is unsettled enough without subjecting it to experimental hot dogs, so I go with my usual dog, mustard and chopped onions. Google tries it just like that, though, with olives and pineapple, and loves it. He compliments my dad in Spanish and makes a thumbs-up sign.

We carry our hot dogs back to the dugout while spectators cheer and reach out to slap my hand in greeting. The bleachers are already packed. More people are gathered beyond the outfield fence.

Channel 4 from Sutton is there to tape highlights of the game for the evening news. A radio van is there, too, with bullhorn-style speakers on the roof. They're going to announce the game later, but for now classic rock is piping out of the speakers. Sturgis stops practicing and talks to the DJ. It's his kind of music, so I'm not surprised.

Bobby tries to inspire us with a few words about the long, noble tradition of Moundville baseball. We even do a little pregame ritual, stacking our hands and shouting, "Moundville! Moundville! Let's go!"

The announcer calls the Sinister Bend team's names first, to scattered applause. Then he reads our names as we come out of the dugout. I feel a thrill when I'm announced as catcher and team captain, batting fourth in the order, and the crowd goes nuts. It's a tremendous feeling, like being in the big leagues. I try to find my mom among the sea of faces, but I can't see her.

We run out onto the field to take our positions. A local singer belts out the national anthem. The mayor throws out the first pitch, and I have to move about a foot right of the plate to catch it on the bounce.

Finally, it's time to play baseball. The roar of the crowd grows louder as Rita throws a few warm-up pitches, and the first Sinister Bend hitter stands on deck and takes a few practice swings. When the batter steps into the box and takes the first pitch for a strike, I wonder if the entire town will simply be swept up into the sky by pure joy and excitement.

The excitement doesn't last long, though. The first batter raps the second pitch into shallow center field for a hit, and the next batter singles to left. Rita panics, walks a batter, and then gives up a double to Peter "the Bat" Labatte. Just like that, the score is three to nothing, and there's still nobody out.

It feels like the inning might go on forever, the Sinister Bend team piling up runs until all of us are old and gray. The crowd gets restless, muttering encouragement that sounds a bit sharper as Rita falls behind the next hitter.

I see P.J. getting careless, taking too long a lead off of second base. I catch Kazuo's attention and fire the ball to him. We have P.J. picked off. The crowd goes wild as he runs back and forth and the ball is tossed back and forth in front of him.

Please don't goof this up! I think just as the runner tries

to dive past Google and touch the bag. Google applies the tag, and a tremendous cheer goes up, shaking the ballpark. The radio van blasts a song called "Been Caught Stealing," with dogs barking, and the Moundville fans join in, barking and stomping on the bleachers.

It changes everything. Rita gets her screwball working, and the next two batters ground out. We go back to the dugout trailing by three but feeling better.

When Sturgis goes out to throw his warm-up pitches in the bottom of the inning, the speakers blare an old hard-rock song.

Outlaw from the badlands baby badlands baby.

"That's his dad's song," says Bobby Fitz. "Ironic, isn't it? I mean, considering what happened to him."

"What's that?"

"They played that song in Baltimore when Carey Nye came out to pitch. It was his theme song, you know, like Mariano Rivera has with that song about the Sandman. All them pitchers have theme songs now."

"Of course." That was why Sturgis went to the radio van. He wanted to put in his request for mound music.

I know the Robinsons are seated right by the dugout, so I pop out.

"Mr. R., can you get the PA guy to play Rita a song? For when she comes to the mound?"

"Sure. Like what?"

"You know music better than I do. Just don't pick anything too weird."

"I have an idea," he says, squeezing past his wife and eighteen other people to run down the bleachers.

"Nothing weird!" I holler after him.

Sturgis quickly strikes out the side. A few minutes later, we're running back out onto the field. I wonder how we're ever going to score four runs on these guys. The radio van blares another old-time rock-and-roll song:

> Foxey! Foxey!
> Now I see you come down on the scene.
> Oh, Foxey.
> You make me wanna get up and scream!
> Foxey!

It's pretty great. The crowd is into it, and Rita is pumped up by it, bouncing around on the mound, throwing her warm-ups with new zip. She gets the first two batters out on ground balls, then strikes out Sturgis to end the inning.

"I can pitch!" she shouts as we go back to the dugout. "Who says I can't pitch? 'Cause I can pitch!"

I lead off in the bottom of the inning. Sturgis throws right at me. I dive, but the ball still clips me in the shoulder. It smarts like anything, and for a split second, I think I'll charge the mound and force-feed him the ball. Instead, I take first, just hoping we can make him pay for putting the leadoff batter on base.

Instead, he strikes out the side.

"He's so amazing," Shannon says as Sturgis saunters off the mound, her eyes misty with emotion.

"The boy can pitch," I agree.

Rita settles down, and for a while, it's a pitchers' duel.

The Sinister Bend team gets a few base runners but doesn't score any more runs (P.J. ends up three-for-three). We get out of trouble with some good pitches and some good plays on defense. The highlight is a triple play started by Google, but it's taken back by the umps, who decide in retrospect that the infield fly rule ought to have been called.

There are no highlights on offense. We're hitless through four innings plus. Our only base runners have been on a hit-by-pitch and an error. Nobody's even gotten to second base.

The highlight for the Sinister Bend team is a strikeout by Sturgis, with me at the plate swinging out in front of what I can only describe as a twenty-six. It's got so much heat it leaves burns on my jersey. Sturgis loses his prosthetic ear on the pitch from the effort. He's still out on the mound, swaying like a scarecrow in a windstorm, one-eared and fragile, long after I've dropped my bat and skulked back to the dugout.

Rita is supposed to lead off in the fifth inning.

"I'm going to have Anthony pinch-hit," I tell her.

"All right," she says.

"I think I'll have someone else pitch the sixth, too. Get a fresh arm out there."

"So you don't need me anymore?"

I don't know how to answer that. It's too loaded with meaning.

"You were amazing," I tell her. She *was* amazing, too, pitching far above her ability on nothing but grit and determination. "But yeah, I guess that means you're done."

"Okay," she says casually, setting the bat aside. I can't tell if she's relieved or disappointed. Then she gives me a big hug, squeezing the life out of me. I can't help but wonder if there's a bit more than team camaraderie to it. I'm redder than the stitches on a baseball when I get back to the dugout.

Anthony digs in, staring down Sturgis. He swings past two fastballs but lifts the third over the shortstop's head. The ball bounces on the grass in no-man's-land. Anthony is so stunned he doesn't leave the batter's box right away.

"Run! Run!"

He does at last and gets to first base just in time to beat the throw. The crowd sends up a deafening roar. We have a hit! We have a base hit!

Sturgis stamps on the mound and wheels around to bark at the shortstop for being out of position. The boy shrugs and takes a few steps back.

Peter walks out to the mound. He hasn't had to do too much as their team manager so far. He talks to Sturgis and calms him down, gives him a friendly pat on the back, and returns to the dugout.

Sturgis fools Miggy on a changeup, striking him out, then stages a long battle with Steve.

Google squints at Sturgis while he pitches to Steve and says something in Spanish.

"He says watch the way the mean boy is breathing," says Miggy, translating.

"Huh?"

Steve manages to draw a full count before swinging over another junkball and striking out. The crowd groans, then groans again: Anthony has taken off on the pitch and is thrown out trying to steal second. So much for our first base hit of the game.

Google is talking excitedly. Miggy shrugs him off.

"I don't know what the big deal is," he tells me. "He keeps talking about how Sturgis breathes."

"No kidding?" I wish I could replay the last inning and see what he's talking about, but it's time to put on the tools of ignorance and squat through one more inning.

We have to juggle the defense a bit, with Rita gone. Kazuo will pitch the last inning, so I move Google to second base and Miggy up to third. I put Anthony in left field. That worries me a bit, since Anthony is a slow runner, but there's not much else I can do.

We're facing the bottom of the order, so I feel okay about Kazuo pitching. He doesn't have any trick pitches, but at least he can throw left-handed to the left-handed batters and right-handed to the right-handed batters. His switch-pitching starts a long talk among the umpires, but they find no rule against it, so they let him do it.

He does give up a leadoff double, but the next two batters fly out to left. My heart stops beating for a moment when Anthony loses the second one in the sun, but Shannon heroically glides in and snatches the ball just before it bops him in the nose. The runner moves up to third on that one.

Sturgis comes up to the plate, and things get a little weird.

First Kazuo nails Sturgis right in the butt. It's obviously intentional. Sturgis glares, and Kazuo glares back.

"Throw at me," Sturgis grumbles as he walks to first.

"Throw at us again and see what happens," shouts Kazuo, kicking the pitching rubber.

The umpires meet again and try to talk while the crowd jabbers and buzzes. Bobby goes out to plead our case to them. Finally, the umps decide to let Kazuo off with a warning.

If that's not weird enough, when Kazuo gets ready to pitch to the next batter, Sturgis walks off the base and heads for the dugout. Kazuo blinks and throws the ball to David. David runs after Sturgis and tags him out in foul territory. (He's out anyway at that point, but David doesn't know it.)

Peter barks at Sturgis while the rest of the team just looks at him in disbelief.

"We have three runs!" Sturgis shouts. "How many do you think we need? Do you think they're going to score four runs on me in one inning?" He grabs his glove, tosses his helmet, and heads for the mound. Peter just shakes his head in sorrow and returns to the dugout.

Sturgis strikes out Tim to start the bottom of the sixth. He's getting tired but is still effective, throwing fastballs mixed with changeups. He takes a deep breath before each pitch and hurls the ball as if it's a fastball. The hitter is always guessing when to swing.

Something about his breathing, I remember. Google noticed something.

I watch Sturgis pitch to Google. He takes a breath and pitches the ball. It's an off-speed pitch, maybe a seven. It's ruled a strike.

Sturgis gets the ball back, takes a deep breath, and pitches. Another changeup, a mite faster. Maybe an eight. Google fouls it off for strike two.

What am I looking for?

Sturgis breathes in slow and deep, then lets the pitch fly.

"Ten!" I shout.

Google flails at the ball and fouls it off.

"He's counting," I tell everyone. "He's counting how fast he's going to throw it."

"Counting?" Anthony asks.

"Yes. He's counting. It's how I taught him to gauge his pitches. He doesn't know he's doing it."

"What?" Kazuo leans in to get a better look at Sturgis.

I pass David in the hole as Google takes a ball.

"Watch him breathe," I whisper. "He counts the speed of his pitches while he inhales. Sit on the changeup."

"Huh?"

"I'll explain in a bit."

I go on deck and tell Shannon. She gives Sturgis a side-long glance and nods.

Google takes a time-out. He looks at me curiously.

I point at my nose, breathe in, and surreptitiously point at Sturgis. Google smiles and nods, which means he knows all about it. He's just waiting for the pitch he wants.

Sturgis takes a breath—I count to six—and pitches. Google times it right, getting the barrel of the bat out to lay down a bunt. The third baseman is too far back to play it, and Sturgis doesn't even come off the mound. Google speeds to first. The crowd stands up and cheers.

"He counts the speed of his pitch!" says David in sudden comprehension.

"It'll still be hard to hit," I tell him. "But it's something to go by."

Shannon goes to the plate, watching Sturgis carefully. He takes a long, deep breath—a ten, at least—and fires. She takes the pitch for a strike.

Sturgis gets the ball back, takes a quicker breath, and lets go.

Shannon swings, connecting solidly, chopping the ball over his head. She makes it safely to first, and Google gets safely to second.

Sturgis wheels around and glares at his shortstop again.

It's not his fault, I think. Don't look at him. Don't be like your old man.

Peter walks out to the mound again. This time there's no friendly pat on the back. He just says a few words, Sturgis snaps something in retort, and Peter stalks back to the dugout.

Sturgis shakes it off, takes a deep breath, and pitches to David.

David sits on the changeup, taking a couple of faster pitches until Sturgis barely takes a short breath and lobs a soft one at him. You can see David's eyes widen as the grapefruit comes to him, and he knocks the juice right out of it. The ball skips past the shortstop to shallow left field.

Google flies around third and scores. When P.J. throws the ball all the way home from left field, Shannon moves up to third base and David moves on to second. The Moundville fans stomp and roar and whistle. The radio van blares that it's been a long time since we rocked and rolled, which it has. Far too long, the crowd seems to think.

Sturgis is visibly shaken, looking from fielder to fielder, wondering who to blame for this new disaster. I almost feel sorry for him.

Peter takes a few steps out on the field, but Sturgis waves him back to the dugout.

When Kazuo comes to the plate, Sturgis just snorts and throws a fastball at his stomach. Kazuo jumps back, letting the ball graze his shirt. It's just enough to take first base and not enough to hurt.

The umpires convene again. Peter doesn't even bother arguing with them, but they just decide to let Sturgis off with a warning. One more hit batter and he'll be gone.

I've barely had my time on deck, so I dawdle getting into the batter's box, taking practice swings and thinking about the speed of his various pitches. I'm not going to sit on the changeup, though. I'm going to sit on the fastball. I'll end this thing here and now, with one swing of the bat. Anything hit hard and fair can clear the bases and win the game.

I go to the plate, all business. Sturgis glares at me, and I stare back coldly, waiting for the pitch. We aren't brothers or cousins or friends, my look tells him. Right now we're enemies, and your back is against the wall.

He takes a deep breath. I count and know it's the pitch I want. He lets go, so I swing for the fences. I connect, hard, and the ball flies off the bat, carrying with it the hopes and dreams of thousands of fans as it soars into the summer sky.

Chapter 22

The celebration is held at the pizza parlor across the street. Bobby Fitz and Mr. Robinson treat us to pizza and ice cream, and there's loud, happy music playing, and an indescribable feeling of exuberance fills the air. The place is jammed to the rafters with people wanting to join in the fun. My dad is the only one missing. He had to get the tent and everything back to Sutton.

"You're the toast of Moundville," Mr. Robinson tells me when the umpteenth family comes by to shake my hand.

So I didn't smash the scoreboard and circle the bases in slow motion in a shower of sparks, but my double cleared the bases and scored the go-ahead run. That was good enough for me.

"Heck, he's the toast *and* the jam," says Rita.

"I think you're pretty jamming yourself, Foxey Lady," I tell her. Our relationship has changed all at once into knowing looks and flirty comments and accidental touches. Whatever hesitation Rita had about being my girlfriend seems to have ended at the exact time we stopped being teammates. I'm having fun, but I'm also sort of in knots about it. I drink a gallon of root beer, but my mouth is still dry.

"She definitely digs you," Anthony whispers to me when Rita takes a little break from the table. That's what scares me, I think. He's got an easier role, admiring Shannon from afar. I'm in a position where I have to actually do something.

I realize Shannon is missing. I wonder if she's gone off to celebrate with her family separately or if maybe she's just anxious about the first day of school tomorrow.

"What happened to Shannon?" I ask Rita when she gets back.

"I don't know," she says. She shrugs just a little bit too theatrically for me to believe her, but Shannon's secrets don't interest me that much.

When I get up myself, I see my mom wedged into a corner booth full of moping Sinister Bend fans. There's a few empty pitchers of beer on the table.

"That was a great game, kid," she tells me. She stands up awkwardly to give me a smooch and tousle my hair. I'm glad there's a throng of people between us and the rest of the team.

"Are you going to be around much longer?" I ask her.

"I'm afraid not, kid," she says. "I'm taking a red-eye to Boston so I can work a flight to Dublin tomorrow."

"Well . . . ," I tell her. But whatever people say in these cases doesn't make it out. Have a nice flight? Have a nice life?

"I was on my way to the, uh." I gesture toward the restrooms.

"All right," she says. "Hey, you guys be good. Both of you, you're extraordinary."

When I'm washing my hands in the restroom, it occurs to me to wonder, Does she mean me and Sturgis, or me and my dad?

There's no paper towels left, so I shake my hands dry and head back for my table. My mom and her friends are gone.

Nobody's forgotten that school starts the next day, so even though the whole town was packed into the pizza place, by nine o'clock the restaurant starts to empty.

"I'll see you soon," Rita tells me when her parents come to collect her. She surreptitiously passes me a napkin with her cell phone number.

"See you," I tell her casually. I fold the napkin and put it neatly into my pocket. "I guess I'll head out, too."

"You need a ride?" Bobby asks.

"It's a short walk," I tell him. I figure a few moments of fresh air and solitude will do me good . . . clear my head and everything.

As soon as I step outside, I notice a brisk wind has picked up. It's like the weather knows that summer is over and school's starting. Someone comes toward me, silhouetted against the lights, and for a very weird second I think it's the ghost of Ptan Teca coming to get me.

"Hey, Roy," the ghost says. A chill goes through me. I know better than to believe in ghosts, but it's a spooky moment.

Then I realize it's just P.J.

"Hey." We slap hands like old friends.

I wonder if he's moping around so he won't have to face his dad. A decent left fielder might have caught the ball I hit to left or at least thrown it back into the infield to keep

Kazuo from scoring the go-ahead run. He seems to be taking it well, though.

"It was fun today," he tells me. "Great game. I love a good rundown. Nice hit at the end, too."

"Thanks."

"I know I'm supposed to be miserable, but I'm not. So we lost." He shrugs. "My dad just takes it so seriously."

"Yeah, I know. He's a good guy, though. Maybe a little obsessed with baseball, but who isn't?"

"Yeah, well . . . it's not just baseball to him," he says. "He thinks he can, like, set things right. Avenge the past. Appease the spirits. He thought if we beat you guys, maybe it would settle something once and for all."

"So what happens now?"

"Who knows?" He shrugs. "Probably the end of the world."

"It was the double of doom." I do my best Darth Vader voice, which isn't very good. We laugh until a particularly icy blast of wind hurls down Main Street and sucks the humor out of both of us.

"Hey, you got a ride home?" Not that I can help him if he does need a ride.

"I usually find a way," he says, and nods at me before walking on, looking a bit like a ghost again before he disappears into the shadows.

He's a weird duck, I think, but I'd still love to have that kid in my lineup.

I notice a kind of swirling dusty whiteness in the street-lights.

"I think it's snowing," I announce to no one in particular. It hasn't snowed in Moundville since before I was born. It has only rained, even when it snowed all around us. Now it's snowing on September 4. Whatever angry spirits or meteorological oddities brought on the rain aren't finished yet. Maybe Ptan Teca was just taking a little break and is back for more.

I don't know how long I stand there watching it. I'm hypnotized. It's so beautiful and silent, and I feel as if I'm in a snow globe.

When I get home, my dad is crashed out in an armchair, watching the evening news. They're showing the highlights of the game.

"It's the hero of the hour!" He jumps up and gives me a bear hug.

"Thanks," I tell him when I can finally breathe again.

"They're replaying the whole thing on Channel 54. It's nearly done, but I'm taping it for you. I'll dump it on DVD later. You'll want this forever." He looks tired and smells of charred hot dog. "Sorry I didn't make the party."

"I know you had to do stuff," I tell him. "Did you sell a lot of hot dogs?"

"Not enough to send you to St. James, but I can pay the bills this month."

"Good enough for me," I tell him. "Hey, how is Sturgis doing?"

"You mean he's not with you?"

"The losing pitcher doesn't usually go to the victory party," I tell him. "I figured he was with you."

"That's weird," he says thoughtfully. "Hey, Shannon's parents called an hour ago. She's missing, too. You don't suppose they're hanging out somewhere, do you?"

"I don't know." I think about the day Rita and Shannon came over to visit, when Sturgis wasn't home. Rita making room in Mrs. Obake's SUV so Sturgis could ride home with Shannon. Shannon near tears when Sturgis quit the team and misting up again today when she watched him pitch. Rita acting mysterious about Shannon's whereabouts after today's game.

Every one of those times, I was too preoccupied with myself and baseball and Rita to think about an obvious alternative.

"Chicks dig scars," I say.

"Huh?" says my dad.

"I bet they're together," I tell him.

"Well, I guess I better go look for 'em," my dad says. He gets up and heads for the front door.

We take a quick drive around the town. The snow fills the canals and sweeps across fields of mud that have just become stubbly with new grass. The baseball field, where there was so much noise and excitement earlier, is now a soft white blanket. The new bleachers look like they came with long white cushions.

"There's no footprints," my dad points out.

"Well, they've been there for a while."

He pulls over and parks. We cross the snowy field toward the dugouts. You can't see anything in the shadows, but I think I hear someone trying not to be heard.

"Sturgis!" I shout.

"Go away!" he shouts back.

I can see a white face and long hair appear on the dugout steps, but it's Shannon.

"Are you guys all right?" my dad calls.

Shannon walks over to us. She's been crying. Shannon is kind of weepy, I've decided.

"We're fine. He's just embarrassed. He gave up the winning runs, and . . . well, he also made the last out for them. He doesn't want to face you guys."

"You should go talk to him," my dad says, putting his hand on my shoulder. "You're his best friend. Tell him it's no big deal."

"I think you should go," I tell him. "You're sort of his dad now. Anyway, you're his hero."

"You think so?"

"Dad, he loves your cooking and laughs at your jokes. He's read all your books on home improvement. I honestly think he'd rather work for you than play baseball."

My dad looks at the dugout, about as confident as an American League pitcher coming to the plate in a National League ballpark. Finally, he heads over to tell Sturgis that everything is going to be all right, a smile plastered across his face.

To me, that's his defining moment.

They're in there for a long time. Shannon and I go to the other dugout so we can sit down. We sit quietly, Shannon still snuffling.

"Rita kind of likes you," she finally says to break up the silence.

"I know," I tell her. "I like her, too."

That's the extent of our small talk.

At last, Dad and Sturgis come out of the visitors' dugout, Sturgis leading the way. We go out, too, and meet them halfway.

Sturgis scowls at me and knocks my hand away when I offer it to him.

"You got a lucky hit," he says. "Stupid left fielder should have had that."

Then his sneer twists into a smile, and I see he's putting me on.

"Hey, they all look like line drives in the box score," I tell him with a grin. I offer him my hand again, but instead of shaking it, he grabs it and pulls me into a clumsy hug.

"We'll see you in the truck," my dad says. He and Shannon go back across the field, leaving Sturgis and me alone in the baseball park snow globe.

"So you and Shannon, huh?"

"She's nice," he says. "She came and talked to me after the game. One thing led to another."

"I've noticed that happens with girls." Thinking about Rita makes me feel warm, even in the chilly air.

"She's made this whole thing easier, I guess," he admits.

"Bring her to meet your dad. He won't feel so bad about you losing. He'll just brag that his boy is dating the second-hottest girl in town."

He laughs. "Roy, my dad doesn't care about that game anymore."

"What about you, then?" I wonder. "Why did you switch teams? I thought it was for your dad."

"I don't know," he says. "Peter kind of talked me into it, told me it was my duty or my fate or whatever. When you were such a jerk about it, it got easier. I wanted to show you up."

I decide there's no point in arguing over who was a bigger jerk.

"You did show me up," I tell him. "You only lost because of Google." I explain how the pint-sized third baseman noticed how Sturgis was tipping his pitches. "You got solved, but it wasn't by me. I just reaped the benefits."

"Can you fix it in time for Sutton Junior High to beat St. James Academy JV in the spring?" he asks.

"We'll work on it."

When we get up the next morning for our first day of school, we learn that all the schools are closed in Sutton and Mound

County on account of the snow. It's national news. Nowhere in the history of the United States, not even in North Dakota or Alaska, was the first day of school ever called on account of snow before.

Sturgis and I head down to the ballpark, just on a whim. Shannon and Rita are already there, and the four of us build a snowman on the pitcher's mound, looking back over his head in anguish as an imaginary baseball flies past him.

Pretty soon we're joined by Steve, David, Kazuo, and the others. Google has never seen snow before and is beside himself with wonder, making snow angels in the outfield. Eventually, we're joined by other people in town. Even Dad is there; he's taken the day off work.

We populate the field with snow players, re-creating the last play of the game yesterday. We load the bases and set the runners in motion. We put all the Sinister Bend defenders out on the field. Someone uses a long stick to place a snowball in midair a foot above the webbing of the snowman left fielder's glove. We line up snowmen along the Moundville dugout, waiting for the chance to bat.

Finally, we build the snowman batter. Rita gives the batter such a round-eyed and goofy expression that we all laugh until our stomachs hurt. Even when we're done, I still hear a kind of echo of laughter on the icy wind.

When the snow stops, the deep cold settles in, putting a frosty glaze on everything. It's like living in a freezer. The smart part of me thinks it's my imagination, while some other part of me—the part that believes in luck instead of percentages—thinks it's Ptan Teca after all, exacting his cold revenge from the spirit world.

The thing is, if I could do it over again, I would do exactly the same thing. I don't care if there's a whole new ice age coming and Moundville is trampled to dust by woolly mammoths. I'm going to swing at that pitch *every time*, no matter what happens.

I've read on the Internet that Moundville now has the record for most consecutive days below freezing, at least outside the Arctic and Antarctic circles. So if you happen to drive by, be sure to stop at the ballpark. You can see our snowpeople, acting out the last at bat that was ever played there.

You can see it there, literally frozen in time: my own defining moment.

Acknowledgments

I want to thank all the people who helped nudge me and *Mudville* along:

- My wife, Angela, for encouraging me to take this project up again, and for always being willing to read and reread pages hot off the printer (even after she'd gone to bed).
- The old friends who were the least surprised to learn I'd made this dream come true, including Terry Aman, Nathan Irwin, Tony Kiendl, and Colette Lunday Brautigam.
- Readers of the first few drafts, including Jim Anderson, Amanda Coppedge Bosky, Amy Brenham, Gillian Chan, Brad Cohen, Megan Meyers, Jennifer McNeil, and Giuliano Kornberg.
- Batgirl, for her brilliant baseball writing, and her close personal friend, Anne Ursu, for her excellent advice and support.
- Tina Wexler, for guiding me through the publishing world.
- Allison Wortche and the other wonderful people at Knopf.
- Lisa Elbert, for sharing her expertise of Dakota language and culture.
- Noam Kritzer, whose kindness compelled me to rethink my positions on both lawyers and Yankees fans.
- My favorite baseball writer, Mark Harris, who casts a shadow on every page of this novel.

Also by Kurtis Scaletta

When his dad gets a job at the U.S. embassy in Liberia, twelve-year-old Linus Tuttle knows it's his chance for a fresh start. Instead of being his typical anxious self, from now on he'll be cooler and bolder: the new Linus.

But as soon as his family gets off the plane, they see a black mamba—one of the deadliest snakes in Africa. Linus's parents insist mambas are rare, but the neighborhood is called Mamba Point, and Linus is sure the venomous serpents are drawn to him—he can barely go outside without tripping over one. Then he hears about kasengs—and the belief that some people have a deep, mysterious connection to certain animals.

Unless Linus wants to hide in his apartment forever (drawing or playing games with the strange kid downstairs while his older brother meets girls and hangs out at the pool), he has to get over his fear of his kaseng animal. Soon he's not only keeping a black mamba in his laundry hamper; he's also feeling braver than ever before. Is it his resolution to become the new Linus, or does his sudden confidence have something to do with his scaly new friend?

From Kurtis Scaletta comes a humorous and compelling story of a boy learning about himself through unexpected friends, a fascinating place, and an extraordinary animal.

Available from Knopf, Summer 2010